NIGHTMARE PRESS
PRESENTS

ANIMAL
UPRISING!

Nightmare Press
Louisville, KY

ANIMAL UPRISING!

Thank you for reading! If you like the book, please leave a review on Amazon and Goodreads. Even if you don't like it, please still leave a review.

To keep up with more Nightmare Press news, join the Anubis Press Dynasty on Facebook.

TABLE OF CONTENTS

INTRODUCTION: UP RISE THE ANIMALS!

ABOUT THE AUTHORS

INTRODUCTION: UP RISE THE ANIMALS!

Prior to writing *Night of the Possums,* some of the people I had mentioned the book idea to expressed how much they liked animal horror. After we released it, a lot of people started talking to us about how much they liked the concept of the book and how they felt there just wasn't enough animal horror out there. The book began to receive a lot of positive feedback and readers started asking me if I was going to write a sequel. This sparked a lot of lengthy and enjoyable conversations about animal horror. Come to find out, there are a lot of fans of that particular subgenre.

So, this gave Jenny and me an idea: let's make the first Nightmare Press anthology animal horror themed. We thought, "Hey, there's bound to be a few people with some frightening stories of killer creatures to tell. Let's see what happens." Boy, we had no idea.

A few? Yeah, there were a lot more than that.

Almost as soon as we made the announcement, the Nightmare Press inbox was blowing up with submissions. Every day it seemed a few new stories came in (most days saw quite more than a few), and soon we were fighting our way through a ton of animal horror stories while simultaneously working to get our Anubis Press anthology, *Paranormal Encounters,* completed. We had no idea so much interest in the animal horror anthology had been generated. So many submissions were sent that we actually had to step back and let the deadline run out before we could really dig in.

When we finally dug in we came across many great stories. Narrowing them down was difficult and took a lot of time and consideration. We had to make some really tough decisions. In the end, we had to look at keeping a balance. We didn't want too many dog stories or too many insect stories. We received an abundance of stories about spiders and cats. Some submissions were really good tales but they just weren't what we were looking for. Others weren't even animal horror. It took a lot of time, but we finally narrowed it down to those we thought best fit the theme and also kept a good balance, bringing a variety of not only animals but writing styles as well. In the end, even though we had to pass on so many great submissions, we feel we pieced together a wild and well-written collection of creepy, sophisticated, frightening, and bone-crunching animal horror stories.

We'd like to thank every single author who submitted a story. Writing is hard work and a labor of love, and each author puts so much into their work. We appreciate everyone who was willing to trust us with their stories. That means a lot. Thank you for thinking of us.

And especially thank you to the readers who have awaited the completion of this work, and those who read *Night of the Possums* and gave us the idea to do this. Thank you to everyone who has picked this book up to read it. Without you, this entire anthology wouldn't even matter.

So, without further adieu, get comfortable, turn off the lights, and make sure to close your doors until they click shut, because you never know what might wander into your room while you're busy wondering what these animals will do next. There are plenty of hungry and angry critters lurking in the pages ahead. Can you make it to the final page with all your fingers intact? Guess we'll just have to wait and see.

Enjoy the animal uprising you're about to unleash.

Jacob Floyd
Editor

THE GOAT
Michelle Mellon

The goat says: "Where there is blood, there is plenty of food." --Ghanaian proverb

Aiysha didn't notice the goat at first. She was a city girl, and everything about her new farmland surroundings was foreign and overwhelming. Eleven months from turning legal, with a new solicitation conviction, and she was back in the system with a choice: juvenile detention center confinement or live-and-work detail.

She had no experience with farms other than what she occasionally saw on old TV shows. She figured dealing with some bumbling hayheads would be an easy ticket to escape. It wasn't until she'd been on the bus for an hour, wondering how the world could be so empty outside the city, that Aiysha began to doubt her reasoning.

When they finally pulled up to the farm, she was amazed that there were no fences, security gates, or guards. Not that much security was needed for the middle of nowhere. She could see to the horizon in any direction and the scenery was the same shade of nothing.

Cows, goats, sheep, chickens. Her first impression was an overwhelming sea of animals that made the worst piss-corner summer stench in the city pale in comparison. The goat didn't stand out, not then. He was just a faceless bleat in a horrible country chorus. Aiysha wondered what everyone would do if she just climbed back onto the bus and refused to get off again until they were back in the city.

But it's not like there was any real hope for her there. No one cared about one more desperate brown-skinned girl living on the streets. She was tired of scouting covered stoops and niches where she could sleep safely. She was tired of being so hungry that it was better to go without food than have a meal and crave more when there was no possibility for more. And she was tired of being desperate, beaten, and dragged down, running from one pimp's promises straight into the arms of another.

The drugs helped, for a while. They transported her to a nothingness much like the fields surrounding the farm, only soft and serene without the smells and sounds of other living beings. But Aiysha didn't like to lose control, and she didn't like to depend on people who were always going to let her down. So she got sober and remained miserable and lost amongst the rest of the city's walking dead.

The farm turned out to be the opposite. She had her own room, with a vermin-free mattress that was not just cloth over a frame that was missing its padding. She had three meals a day, heaped onto plates served at a table instead of out of soggy paper bags in an alley squat.

She was one of four girls, always dressed in clean, undamaged clothes. They had been entrusted to the care of a widow who was clearly fighting the loneliness following her husband's suicide, and the bitterness of never having children of her own.

The widow was one of the first people to listen to her—to say her name in one smooth, breathy smile instead of adding an extra "ee" syllable like a braying donkey. That earned her Aiysha's grudging appreciation and attention.

The other girls had less patience and fewer capabilities. One was a thief and recovering addict whose drug use had worsened a genetic tremor condition. One was a hacker and presumed hypochondriac whose phantom pains turned out to be a high-risk pregnancy. And one was a violent offender with a short fuse.

So Aiysha usually drew the duties that involved direct contact with the animals: milking, collecting eggs, administering medicine. At first, she was terrified, but after a few months she had grown proud of her caretaking abilities. That was when she noticed the goat.

She always collected the eggs first, milked the cows, then milked the goats. Normally she was in and out, performing her chores with single-mindedefficiency so she could earn TV time before the other girls claimed the set. But the cable had been out for a few days and Aiysha was in no mood for one of the widow's Bible readings, so she dawdled at each stage, studying all the animals in turn.

The billy goat stood apart in the pen. It was not a big space, so the empty circle of air around him was quite noticeable. Aiysha felt, rather than saw, the other goats' reluctance to move closer to him. He, in turn, seemed stubbornly indifferent to their reaction.

She laughed a little, putting herself in his place. If he had been Aiysha in her earlier days, he'd stand there with his lips tucked and his arms crossed and his eyes squinty like shutters to keep out the rest of the world. Instead, he was just a stubborn goat that probably smelled weird or kicked or bit or for some simple reason just didn't fit with the other goats.

Although she recognized some irony in the situation, Aiysha figured it was best to follow the instinct of the herd. She didn't know the animals well enough to know what else to do. Keeping a safe distance, she glanced the goat over to make sure he wasn't wounded or looking ill, then moved on to finish the rest of her chores.

In the middle of the night, Aiysha woke up to a different room. The roof was sloped, and she was on the top level of a bunk bed with the peeling ceiling paint just inches above her head. Below, she heard someone crying. She rolled to the edge of the bed and looked over.

There was no one there.

A shadow darkened the window at the head of the bottom bunk. Aiysha slipped to the floor. She saw the horns and high sloping forehead of the billy goat. Its eyes were wide and black and looking directly into hers.

Aiysha took a step back and tripped and fell over a long-forgotten toy. The hard-headed soft-bodied doll gaped at her, mocked her, dared her to...she didn't know what. By the time she clambered to her feet and looked back to the window, the goat was gone.

She woke up again in her room on the farm. The dream had seemed so real. She trembled at the memory of her old room in her old life. That time seemed so far away; she had lived a whole other life between then and where she was now.

There was a time in that slope-ceilinged room when she felt safe and strong and someone looked up to her. Long before she was orphaned, before she became a foster kid, before she lost her bottom bunkmate—the sister whose existence Aiysha had buried 10 years earlier, when the tiny broken girl had been lowered into the ground.

After that, after she bounced from one home to another, each worse than the last, Aiysha learned it was easier not to feel, not to care, not to be human. And it served her—not well, perhaps, but enough.

Aiysha felt differently now, here on the farm. She wasn't healed or whole, but she realized she was…happy. In moments. Taking care of the animals. Talking to the widow when there wasn't the weight of the Bible between them. Walking the fields that only months before she'd seen as endless and uninteresting. She feared the dream had come to show her it was something she couldn't have for very long.

It was B Day.

Aiysha had dubbed it that in her head, not sure herself if the B was for "baby" or "birth." But the widow had told them they would all attend, and so they crowded into the hacker's bedroom, waiting on the midwife and doctor since it was too risky to make the long drive to the hospital once labor had started.

The widow was hovering, alternating between murmuring nonsense words of encouragement, wiping the girl's brow, and consulting her Bible, which lay on the wide windowsill. Aiysha tried to stay out of her way, and ended up standing in the doorway, ready to run down the stairs to answer when the midwife and doctor rang.

The thief pressed herself into the corner away from the door and windows, flinching each time the girl on the bed cried out. And the violent girl, the one Aiysha had come to think of as The Dark Girl despite her milky skin, white-blond hair, and green-tea eyes, stood on the opposite side of the bed, trying not to smile at her housemate's obvious agony.

A spot of blood appeared on the sheet below the girl's thrashing legs. Before Aiysha could say anything about it to the widow, it spread into a lake fed by a steady river of red. Then the pregnant girl started screaming, and Aiysha fled seconds later at the welcome sound of the doorbell.

She returned to the room with the midwife, who was just as surprised as all of them that the doctor had not yet arrived. The room smelled of sweat and fear, and the midwife barked an order for towels to cover the stained sheets. Only Aiysha and the thief complied.

By the time they returned, the bleeding had slowed, and the girl lay limply on the bed with her face turned to the window. She was muttering alternately in English and Spanish, and her eyes were focused on something far, far away.

The midwife displayed determination on her face, but defeat was already finding its place in the set of her shoulders. She asked, begged, scolded the girl to push, until finally a sticky pale creature was pulled from between the girl's unmoving legs.

The baby was covered in bits of blood. It looked slimy, alien, and blue. The midwife patted its tiny back and breathed into its tiny nose and mouth, then quickly pulled out and tossed aside a dark ball of mucus. But the baby never breathed.

The mucus landed on the thief's foot. The thief took in the glob and the stillborn baby and the dead girl on the bed (whom the widow had hastily covered with a sheet) and began trembling violently. She managed to push herself further into the corner, outside the immediate orbit of the gloomy scene. The midwife placed the tiny body on the bed and covered it with a towel, so she could help the widow tend to the thief and her growing seizure.

The Dark Girl looked around the room rapturously at all the chaos, then inched closer to the two bodies on the bed; both featureless in their shrouds, one a miniature of its mother. She had not noticed what Aiysha had long-since seen—the face of the goat filling the lower half of one of the room's narrow windows.

As The Dark Girl slyly lifted the sheet and gazed in awe at the larger corpse, Aiysha turned to the goat. She knew it was somehow responsible; knew it was trying to get her attention by flexing and showing its power.

She was confused and afraid. She didn't know what the goat wanted or why. But she knew she didn't want to leave this place and she didn't want to die. So Aiysha glared, pouring every bit of fear and anger she felt into her look.

The goat opened its mouth as if to bray, but there was no sound, just the impression of a smile before it disappeared.

B Day. Breathtakingly Bad. Barbarically Bloody. Biblical Battle Beginning.

Days passed. Then weeks. Aiysha had stopped holding her breath, and the widow's grief had lessened. The other two girls seemed unaffected, and Aiysha suspected that they, like her, were happy to maintain an emotional as well as physical distance from one another.

Things were quiet once again, until the widow began to notice things missing around the house. Trinkets, to be sure, but old and potentially valuable. Although nothing was said directly, Aiysha was moved to indoor duties and the thief was rotated out to barnyard maintenance.

Contrary to everyone's fears, the work seemed to be good for her. Her limp brown hair took on a luster, her thin limbs grew wiry, she lost the dark shadows around her eyes, and her spasms came less frequently.

It turned out The Dark Girl had a penchant for numbers. She spent her days busily sifting through the widow's finances and tax records to get them in order. That left Aiysha the work of cleaning, in which she found a new passion: polishing the widow's antique furniture.

Neglect had left the large wooden relics looking distressed, but not in that carefully contrived way that made people with money pay more for it. Aiysha found she could give the pieces new life as she rubbed oil into cracks and wiped down the scrolls and leaves of carefully carved corner embellishments.

She would save them, because she herself had been given a second chance and knew the feeling that came from being redeemed.

Not the same could be said for the thief. When weeks passed and no more items went missing from the house, the widow's suspicions were justified. She went through the thief's belongings and found evidence the girl was planning to run away. Aiysha watched the widow stalk off to the barn to confront the girl. Minutes later she ran out there herself when she heard the screaming.

The widow knelt next to the girl, who lay still on the ground. Her eyes were rolled back into her head, blood trickled from both nostrils, and her fingers were clenched like claws, leaving gouges in the hay and dirt floor. The pitchfork she'd been using lay to the side, and the pile of hay in one of the stalls had been disturbed just enough to reveal some of the widow's missing heirlooms.

Aiysha stooped beside the still-shrieking widow to check for a pulse. As she turned to look at the girl's contorted face, Aiysha saw it at the end of the barn, standing in the open doorway. The goat nodded at her, bared its teeth, and walked away.

The emergency crew said the girl must have died immediately following her seizure; there was nothing the widow or Aiysha could have done. An investigator came from the state. She talked to the widow and Aiysha and The Dark Girl. No blame was assessed, but because the widow was showing signs of failing health herself, and two girls had died there within months of each other, she would receive no new wards.

Aiysha was given the option to spend the last remaining months of her sentence in the city. She refused, as did The Dark Girl, whose only other option was incarceration in a less-welcoming secured facility.

It worked, for a while. As well as it ever had. And Aiysha began to think of the future. Daydreams about where she might go, what she might do, she even wondered what would happen to the widow and The Dark Girl and the farm. For the first time in a long time she felt an anxious hope.

Aiysha had just finished feeding the animals one morning when she thought she heard voices. She walked toward the house and, through the open kitchen window, heard the widow pleading for her life.

From the sill Aiysha could see The Dark Girl brandishing a knife with one hand while trying to pull that hand back with the other. Aiysha gasped, and the girl turned toward her; a falter just long enough for the widow to scurry backwards out of the kitchen and lock herself in the hallway powder room.

The knife in The Dark Girl's hand began a slow turn, and by the time Aiysha ran inside to meet her in the kitchen, the girl had the knife pointed at her own throat. Her only sounds were whimpers. Her hair was plastered to her forehead and temples like a fair and delicate helmet, and the sweat of her struggle dripped past her wide eyes.

She was so tense Aiysha was sure she would crack into hundreds of pieces and fall, scattering herself across the waxed linoleum floor. For the first time since her arrival 10 months earlier, Aiysha held The Dark Girl's gaze.

I know this isn't you, she told her with her eyes.

Just as she expected, a shadow appeared in her peripheral vision, through the open window. The Dark Girl looked beyond Aiysha and blanched. Aiysha moved so she could block the girl's view of the goat.

She stretched her hand out, palm up, toward the knife. She could see the girl's hands shaking; one clawing desperately again to pull back on the other, the hand with the knife teasing as it began to flop forward and back, nicking the girl's throat in alternating strokes.

Aiysha darted in and reached out with both hands. The edge was up and out and sliced her palms as she tried to close her hands on the weapon. She cried out in pain and in the struggle The Dark Girl stumbled, tripping and falling backward in the kind of slow motion that only precludes disaster.

Arms held stiffly in front of her, knife once again facing her, The Dark Girl hit the floor and her head bounced back up, impaling her throat on the unyielding blade. Aiysha fell to her knees and reached for the girl, but her green eyes were already dull and unseeing. Aiysha knelt beside her, refusing to turn and look even when she felt the goat move away.

Aiysha lay still in her bed, having given up on sleep. In a week she'd be heading back to the city. The death of The Dark Girl had removed any question of whether she had a choice any longer.

It was the beginning of the end, she thought at first, then amended it. It was the middle of the end. Returning to the city would finish it all for her, she had no doubt. She had not only lost her edge, but she didn't want it back. She wanted the girl she had been long before, the young woman she was now, and the woman she was yet to become.

The widow had shrunk to near invisibility. Each girl gone diminished her that much more, and Aiysha felt that with her own departure the widow was certain to vanish.

She closed her eyes and tried to catch a glimpse of that life she'd carved out in her head. Of staying on to help the widow tend the animals and the farm and the thirsty wood. Of going back to school and moving forward, onward, upward, making the widow proud, making herself proud, making the scant memories of her family from before proud.

It was then that she heard it, for the first time. Its voice sounded like she would have expected. Rough and raspy like pushing sound through a mouth full of roaring wind and jagged rock.

I've waited so long for one as right as you, it said. *Sad but strong, lonely but willful, smart but hopeful.*

Aiysha could see the other girls, then. Not just her hapless housemates, but the many girls who came before, scattered across the decades in lonely trickles or random swells.

She saw how she never would have won against the goat with The Dark Girl; could never have come close to winning. She had fallen fully into its trap. In her naïve attempt to intervene, she now had blood on her hands and felt bound by complicity to help the horrid creature.

Aiysha awoke with the crust of tears on her face. One of her bandaged hands held a note with a crude drawing of the widow and a recipe she didn't recognize. But it was clear that both the drawing and the recipe, though shaky, had been written in her own hand.

Over the next couple of days Aiysha kept herself busy helping the widow sell off the larger livestock and pack up her personal belongings. The widow had listed the farm for sale, complete with furnishings and the smaller animals, and decided to retire to a small and anonymous existence away from the woes of the past year. Aiysha quickly came to dread the sight of cars slowing at the For-Sale sign on the far end of the farm.

After a little digging, she learned the recipe she had written was for poison. It had been from her dream, and written in her hand, but she knew its source. The goat seemed to have filled the background spaces in her life and was crowding out the remainder until she feared there'd be nothing left.

There was little about the widow's Bible study that ever interested Aiysha, but strangely she found herself thinking about a passage from Matthew:

Then shall the Kings say unto the goats on the left, "Depart from me, you who are cursed, into everlasting fire prepared for the devil and his angels."

ANIMAL UPRISING!

Unless it was all in her head (and Aiysha had begun wondering, half-hoping that she had created this fiction to fix something deep and broken within), the goat had a plan and a purpose for her. If it truly was evil—demonic, even—could she really resist it? And even if she could, for how much longer?

It turned out interest in the farm was lower than expected, and Aiysha negotiated a two-week extension on her transfer to the city so she could help the widow continue to make arrangements. Although she was able to hurry through her outdoor chores with so many fewer animals to attend to, the goat made it a point now to meet her at the fence. She avoided its gaze, but she could feel its eyes on her the entire time, and knew it watched her long after she was gone.

Nights were the worst time. Aiysha's unfettered sleep was continually interrupted by the widow's loud moaning and muttering. Unwillingly, she suffered through the other woman's nightmares that were surely a gift of the goat. Aiysha was beginning to think the way it wanted her to think—killing the old lady would be a mercy.

Once again it was one week to go, and Aiysha was now plagued not only by the widow's night terrors, but by her own visions. But these were dreams, not nightmares.

They came complete with softened edges; happy blurry reminiscences of a life she had yet to live. The goat showed her how it could be if she obeyed. How she could take over the farm and bring in visitors to feed its need. A steady stream of unsuspecting victims where the occasional disappearance was easily explained away.

It wasn't selfish to want a life for herself, she reasoned in the daylight. The life she had been denied, the kind of life she was owed after what she'd been through. A life of peace and quiet purpose. She could set an example for others like her, show them they didn't have to be lost forever.

But what if she did what the goat demanded? Wouldn't she, in fact, be forever lost, even as she tried to find a new way for herself?

She struggled with the paradox for a few days. The widow grew alarmingly frail, and the goat sent Aiysha his temptation not only in her dreams, but her daydreams as well. She frequently found herself glaring at the shuffling, gasping widow-shroud before her and thinking: mercy.

When the widow fell and Aiysha found herself tending to her every need, she finally snapped. In the moments between fetching tea, water, meals, pillows, pills, and escorting the widow to and from the bathroom, Aiysha pored over the recipe until she had it memorized. She had no long-term plan, just a shortsighted desire to end the mind games and her new servitude.

The day before her departure, Aiysha gathered the ingredients and stood, staring at them on the kitchen counter. Minutes seemed like hours, but even if actual days had passed she didn't think there would be enough time to think things through.

Taking a deep breath, she meticulously prepared the poison. Then, even though the widow was largely confined to her room, Aiysha hurriedly cleaned up the evidence and rushed outside to make the rounds with the animals.

That evening Aiysha sat the widow at the table with cushion and shawl, set a hot mug of tea to one side and a steaming bowl of stew in front of her. She waved off protestation and praise with the assurance that she hadn't gone to that much trouble and it was the least she could do considering everything the generous woman had done for her.

She raised her own mug of tea and made a toast to their last supper. The widow nodded with tiny tears rolling down her cheeks. Although there was still no offer on the farm, she had resigned herself to letting go.

Aiysha sighed inwardly. It was nearly a feeling of contentment. She watched the widow raise a spoonful of stew and mirrored her movements as she blew and blew to cool down her food.

As the widow slid the first portion of stew into her mouth, chewed, smiled, swallowed, and dipped her spoon into her bowl for another taste, Aiysha held her breath. Her own spoon hovered awkwardly near her mouth. A mouth which was busy now telling the widow it was a recipe she dreamed up, complete with fresh herbs from the kitchen garden and a special ingredient to give them both what they needed for the days ahead.

Finally, the scent of homemade sauce and spice and the lure of accompanying fresh-baked biscuits were too much. Aiysha raised her spoon higher in salute to the widow and paused only briefly before she moved it into her mouth.

This was surely the way to go, she thought, appreciating the subtle mix of flavors against her tongue. It was the only way for the two of them to be free.

Aiysha smiled. She could already see the effect the stew was having on the widow. Her face was flushed, her voice high and bright, her hands beginning to tremble.

She had another spoonful herself. She could feel the change coming over her as well. Her vision blurred then refocused, but she couldn't stop grinning. Soon she and the widow would be safe, unreachable, invincible.

She thought about her life here on the farm. She was part of something, belonged somewhere, made a difference. She was no longer sad and lonely and vulnerable. No longer desperate and empty and brittle.

Realizing that had given her the edge she needed to shrug off her despair and fight. The goat was not omniscient, or he wouldn't have eaten the food she gave him, with his own poison hidden within. She had discovered that high heat would neutralize the poison, which made the second part of her plan that much more satisfying.

The widow asked for more, and Aiysha happily refilled her own bowl as well. She did not fear that somehow the evil would be passed to them along with the power. Some part of her knew the malevolence came from within the goat; some kernel of darkness that bloomed fully in the presence of an otherwise benign cosmic power. No, she believed the power alone would come, begetting choices that defined one's true nature.

As she enjoyed her next savory spoonful of homemade goat stew, Aiysha finally felt...joy. She relished that, the pure emotion filling her within. And she looked forward to all the choices she would make in her long life to come.

THE GULL
David Turton

I suffered a most terrible year in 1954. Sales of my debut novel, *The Boat that Sank,* had plateaued to such an extent that my income was non-existent, and I was living on savings. My wife had left me in the summertime, off to travel the world with her lover, Pedro. I don't blame her really, I'm sure I had become insufferable. My mood, my demeanor and my general outlook on life had taken a drastic dip, while my alcohol consumption had flourished.

The main cause of my depression had been writer's block. While writing *The Boat that Sank,* words had flowed from my fingertips like they were being syphoned from somewhere else other than my brain. The joy of discovery as my characters came alive onto the paper, the satisfying sound of my fingers rhythmically tapping out the words on my Remington Typewriter. But, in the whole of 1954, I had only managed to sell two short stories for a total sum of ten pounds. Worse, my second novel just didn't happen. I worked through a dozen iterations but each time I began, I just couldn't see the story through.

So, in mid-January 1955, after the most miserable Christmas of my life, I decided to take my writer's block head-on. I booked a cottage on a most remote island off the North West coast of Scotland, on the advice of Johnny, a hard-drinking Scot from my local pub. The Isle of Faoileag sat between Lewis and St Kilda, a hunk of rock three kilometres by two. Legend has it, according to Johnny, that the island has only ever been inhabited by one man, a recluse who passed away in the latter part of the 19th century. His cottage, the sole building on the island, was now available to rent for the bargain sum of one pound per week.

"Only one catch," Johnny had slurred in this thick, Glaswegian tones, clutching a glass of whisky, "there's nothing there. No shop, no people, no pub. Would send most people mad. But if it's solitude you're after, there's no place like that on the planet. Not a living soul around. Just you and the gulls."

It sounded good to me. A week would be enough, I guessed. Even if I couldn't finish my novel it could give me the push to actually start it, and get a good way through. And if I couldn't write somewhere like that, I couldn't write anywhere. Maybe it could even help me off the drink.

It only took one phone call to someone called Stevie Black, a Scotsman who owns the small cottage and arranges transport to the island. I packed my typewriter and numerous tins of food, and was travelling the next day, a coffee-fuelled twelve-hour drive north from London to the Isle of Skye, where I met Stevie.

"Nutter?" Stevie asked when I first met him and shook his large, rough hand.

"I beg your pardon?" I asked, wondering if I had misheard, unused to the regional accent.

"You one ay these nutters, eh? I see ye type arl the time, lad. Wanna get away from it arl?"

"Something like that. Just want to be by myself for a while, I suppose."

I boarded his boat, and we set sail. Stevie skilfully navigated around the southern tip of Lewis while I dozed on a wooden bench on deck. He wasn't much of a talker and I was glad, especially after a twelve-hour drive. It was six o'clock and darkness had taken hold. I was looking forward to my bed, no matter how hard and uncomfortable it may be.

"There sh'is," Stevie said, pointing. I looked over dozily and saw a grey rock, jutting out of the sea. The strong wind soon brought the world around me into sharp focus. Despite the late hour and the dark sky, I could make out dozens of seabirds flying and circling above the island. As we came closer, I could hear their loud wails alongside the crisp chorus of waves spraying against the rocks below. I shuddered at the noise and turned to see Stevie smiling at me.

"It's their land," he said, pointing at the gulls. They were now close enough to make out the yellow color of their bills, glowing dimly in the pale moonlight. "See ya in a week. Same place, same time. Dinnae forget.

Enjoy yer 'ain comp'ny, lad." The boat turned and soon it was a speck in the distance, rocking on the rough waves.

I walked the half-mile journey to the cottage, using a hand-drawn map that Stevie had provided. The blustery conditions and lack of light made it difficult to find my footing on the rocky surface, but the cottage was the only building on the island, so it didn't take long to find.

As I came to within a few metres of the small wooden door, which was framed by blocks of stone, I looked at the place which was to be my home for the next seven days. Its windows glimmered in the moonlight, the width of them matching the shape of the cottage. The twinkling light on the panes in the darkness gave the cottage a sinister appearance, as if there was something living, aware of my approach. The roof was tiled but in a state of disrepair, covered in crusty white excrement, no doubt from the countless gulls circling overhead. I hoped there were no leaks or holes. Stevie had promised it was in good condition.

I unlocked the door, which opened with a dusty sigh. The cottage itself was even smaller on the inside than it looked from the outside. It consisted of three rooms: a small bedroom, a kitchen and a bathroom. I pulled three candles from my bag and lit them carefully, placing them in each room. The sour smell of the cottage would take some getting used to. I looked over at the bed and saw it had a thin mattress and an old sheet. I groaned, cursing myself that I had only brought two towels and no bedsheets. In any case, I was exhausted. I dropped my bag to the floor and slumped onto the bed, fully clothed. Within thirty seconds I was fast asleep.

I dreamt of screaming children. Several were running toward me on the tiny grey island while waves crashed in every direction, soaking their clothes and their hair. Their screams were loud and in short bursts, shrill and awful, making the hairs stand up on my neck. But the sight of the children was worse than their sound. Each child had no eyes, instead two black chasms sat on their faces, dark red blood oozing down onto their pale cheeks. They were coming towards me, their hands reaching, grabbing, pointing. When I woke abruptly, cold sweat was trickling down my temples. I looked over to the window and saw that the morning light had burst through. A gull screamed above the cottage. Reaching into my bag for my watch, I noticed the time was half past eight. An early enough start.

Ravenous, I opened a tin of tuna and ate it greedily with my fingers, not even waiting to drain the brine. Instead, it leaked down my fingers, the salty smell mixing pleasantly with the hard sea air. I took my typewriter out of the backpack and placed it on the solid wooden table, which sat at the opposite end of the room to the bed, and fed it with paper. I stroked it lovingly. My Remington, the machine that helped change my life in 1952. The vehicle for my story that sold in its thousands. I remember the first cheque in the post for £100. It was a year's salary in one go. Then the next cheque came and by the end of 1953 I had made six hundred pounds. I patted the Remington, with a little more force this time.

"Don't let me down, old boy," I said to it. "We did it before, we can do it again."

I went back to my bag and pulled out tins of tuna, beans, vegetables and corned beef. More than enough for a week. And of course, no alcohol. It would pain me, I knew it would. During the three months it took to write *The Boat that Sank*, I drank whisky every day. The alcohol helped relax my mind, bring up ideas, situations, characters that might have been stuck in a sober mind, without the smooth passage that the lubrication of alcohol allowed. Or so I thought. The problems with my second novel led to more whisky. More whisky led to duller thoughts. Duller thoughts led to poor writing, or none at all. I had lost count of the number of times I'd angrily ripped sheets from the Remington and screwed them up, violently throwing them across the room, yelling, swearing, punching the desk, even throwing my precious typewriter onto the floor at one point. I had falsely credited the whisky with my success, but I had done myself a disservice. It was all me and without alcohol, without distraction, I would be able to find a way to unlock my talent once more.

I glanced out of the window. The cloudy grey sky seemed to beckon me outside. I wrestled with myself. *Too easily distracted*, I scolded. But what better way to get creative juices flowing than a brisk walk in these picturesque surroundings?

I opened the heavy door and closed it behind me, the bitter wind slapping my face. I pulled the key out of my pocket to lock the door and laughed at myself. Who would break in to a cottage on an island which I am the only inhabitant? I replaced the key in my pocket and walked across the island, to the opposite side from which I had landed the previous night.

I froze, the colour draining from my face. A loud, high pitched wail pierced the winter air and I thought back to the dream that had terrified me before I woke. My hand jumped up to my chest in fright, as my heart raced with an intense velocity. I turned sideways to the source of the noise and saw a gull standing on an old column of crumbling stone. Its head was the same height as me in its elevated position, and its bright yellow eyes burned into mine. Its yellow bill hooked downwards, giving the appearance of an angry frown, and I noticed a pink scar on its large, white belly. It swayed slightly in the blistering wind. The gull threw its head back and yelled once more, a blood-curdling scream that seemed to echo across the grey rocks of this desolate island. I looked across and realized it wasn't an echo. Dozens of other gulls were circling over the cottage. My bones ached with a chill, although I wasn't sure whether it was the winter air or fright. I shook the thought away and laughed at myself. *Silly fool! Frightened by a seagull. What else did you expect on a remote island?* I waved at the seagull and it cocked its head in curiosity.

"Thanks for the welcome, Sir. I do hope you will enjoy having me in your beautiful home," I said.

I turned away, laughing harder. As I walked, I looked over to the horizon. There was nothing else around this lump of rock other than the birds. Blue-grey sea filled the landscape, punctuated by patches of white surf. The sound of the waves crashing against the rocks was louder than it had any right to be, the water almost exploding as it met the hard surface. After walking for around five minutes, I became aware of a darkness tingeing the already dim light directly above me. Then, that horrible sound filled the air once more, a loud, sharp scream in short bursts. I turned quickly and looked upwards.

It was the gull. It was swooping, and fast. From less than a metre away I could see its yellow eyes again, they were focused and alert. I ducked and the gull swooped back up, chuntering vocally as it ascended into the murky sky.

"You bastard! Leave me alone!" I shouted, and ran underneath a nearby tree for safety. I stayed there for an hour, carving my name into the bark. Already shaken, a crack of thunder made me jump, and signalled the onset of a heavy shower. With a burst of confidence and energy, I ran back to the cottage. Paranoid, I looked up at the skies after every few steps. It slowed me down, and the rain that was cascading from the dark clouds fell heavily into my face, but the thought of the gull swooping down while I faced the other way was too much to bear. Luckily, the skies were empty. I made it to the cottage and threw myself on the bed, panting heavily with the exertion.

I looked over at the typewriter. *Oh, how I could do with a drink,* I thought to myself. I was a pathetic man, I concluded. A man who came to a deserted island to escape humanity and even here I see demons, enemies waiting to attack me. Maybe the world is too hard a place for a man like me. Even a common bird holds fear and violence in my tortured, broken mind. Most men would have laughed it off, maybe even fought the gull off. But not me, I make it the trigger for an existential crisis. I shook the thought away. *Remember why you came*, I thought to myself, forcefully. I walked over to the typewriter and began to write.

The hours went by and the words flowed. It felt fantastic. Characters formed and began living and breathing through my words. The rhythm of the Remington's keys sang back to me like it was 1952 all over again. Maybe the gull did me a favour. Maybe the big white flying bastard had been the key to unlocking the talent that had been hiding inside me for so long. Two thousand words turned to five thousand, five to ten, and as the sun set into the rough waters of the western side of the island, I had completed twenty five thousand words. I was tempted to write more, but my fingers burned and I needed food. I grabbed a tin of corned beef, stuffing the meat into my mouth, barely pausing to swallow until my mouth was full. As I put the tin in a makeshift bin under the sink, I stopped and stared at the shelf next to it. There was a bottle of whisky, unopened, sitting dustily behind the bin. I placed my hand on my head and ruffled my hair in disbelief. *It would be great to have a drink now*, I thought. I averted my eyes from the bottle. I had been three days without a drink and today was the best day I'd had in over a year. Surely that was a sign to ignore the whisky.

I walked out the kitchen briskly and sat on the bed, wringing my hands. I still wasn't tired but I had decided to leave any further writing until early tomorrow morning. I looked at the wooden door, encased in its stone surroundings, and decided to go for a walk. Darkness had descended on the Isle of Faoileag and the gull would be dozing, or even asleep. Even if it wasn't, I wanted to prove that I was man enough to face it again. It's not like a gull was a deadly animal, after all.

I walked out of the door and looked up. A few gulls glided at the other end of the island, looking like black shapes in the dark blue sky, but none looked too close or ominous. I walked on, deciding to complete a lap of the island. If I walked briskly, it would take less than three quarters of an hour.

I made it thirty minutes and could see the cottage in the distance when I heard the yell, a rasping, guttural screech that could have risen from the pits of Hell itself. I turned to see the descending gull right above my head, but this time I was ready to fight. I clasped my fist around a thin, cold leg. Its screaming became louder and panicked. Yet again I looked into those cold yellow eyes and saw the pink scar on its otherwise pristine white body. Time seemed to slow down as I pulled the leg down toward me. Each wing stretched widely and cut through the moist air as they rapidly moved up and down. I felt a sharp pain at the top of my head and then a warm sensation down my face. The gull had surged forward and jabbed me with its sharp bill. Staggering, I let go of its leg and it soared into the night sky. With one hand on my wounded head I ran clumsily back to the cottage. Less than thirty yards from the door I stumbled on a rock and sprawled comically across the ground, rolling three times before stopping. I shook my head and glanced upwards. The large shadow of the gull was sweeping across the sky; in my daze I saw it as a huge crucifix, ominous and terrible. I might have imagined it but I'm sure, even twenty yards below it on the cold ground, that I could see its evil yellow eyes and its malevolent grimace. It screamed again into the night, its sharp yell causing my hair to stand on end and an icy shiver to run through my whole body. I gathered my senses and clumsily threw myself to my feet. As I reached the front door I heaved it open and fell inside the cottage.

Sweating, despite the bitterness in the air, I looked around the inside of the cottage's stone walls. Was this to be my prison for the next few days? I could not leave until then, surely. I would have to creep out and ensure the gull would not see me. I have no doubt that, if I'd stayed on the ground where I fell, it would have landed on me and used its bill to rip me to shreds.

I lay on the floor panting heavily, my head throbbing. My mind immediately went to the whisky. Three days without a drink was nothing, most people, even relatively hard drinkers, go through that without really thinking. And it could help with the pain. I jumped to my feet and walked over to the bottle. I uncorked it, with some effort, and poured it into a glass. Walking back to the bedroom, I swilled the whisky in the glass, releasing its sweet smell into the air. I sniffed up the fumes and my eyes rolled with pleasure. *I deserve this*, I thought. I sat on the bed and looked at the glass, wanting to savour it, to delay it as long as possible. To hurt myself, tease myself in some way, for some deep psychological reason that I couldn't comprehend. I had been through too much on my short time on this tiny island to regret drinking whisky. As I raised the glass to my lips, closing my eyes as I prepared to taste the thick, sweet liquid, my concentration was broken by the sound of smashing glass. I looked over at the window and felt a freezing gust of wind sting my cheeks. The gull's head emerged through the smashed window. It squeezed through, cutting its white body on the shards of glass, smattering red blood on its white body. It paused and yelled its awful cry, a grisly sound that gave an instant chill to my heart. I froze as it entered the cottage, dropping onto the stone floor below the window.

The gull flapped its huge wings and jumped at me, its talons facing my body. Once more I grabbed its feet and again it thrust its bill forward. I cried in pain as the seagull jabbed me in my right eye, my vision filling with red blood before becoming blurred and dark. I felt blood trickle, warm and wet, down my face.

I looked on in numb shock as I saw my eyeball clasped in the gull's yellow bill, the oozing red blood contrasting with the yellow of its sharp beak. Nonchalantly, the gull flipped my eyeball into its mouth and swallowed. In a bizarre sense of watching the scene from outside my own body, I saw the lump of my eyeball making its way down the bird's throat. Squinting so that the vision out of my remaining eye was as focused as possible, I yanked its feet again, but this only made it angrier. With a violent jerk, the gull plunged its beak into the soft flesh of my stomach. I could feel the intense, searing pain of it grabbing something from inside me and pulling it out. I didn't know what part of me I was looking at as the gull, its face a mess of red gore, emerged with something thick and stringy from a gaping wound in my gut.

Reaching forward painfully, I grabbed the gull's long neck with both hands. I squeezed as hard as I could and heard popping, cracking sounds. I laughed maniacally and stared into those yellow eyes. They were still taunting, mocking me. I screamed into the gull's face and twisted my arms, the extra effort causing my muscles to tighten and strain against my jumper. I released a wild cry of aggression, a warlike scowl that echoed back to me through the smashed window from the misty dark outside the cottage, as the gull's head ripped jaggedly from its body. Crimson blood gushed from its broken body and I threw the evil bird's head down against the stone floor. I sat back, pulled a pillow against the wound in my stomach and laughed. Victory was mine, the enemy crushed with nothing but my own power.

I now know that I will die in this cold, lonely cottage on this cold, lonely island. I'm not really sure how long it takes for infection to set in, but I can smell an awful odour coming from my empty eye socket. It smells tangy, like rotting cheese mixed with almonds. I stopped putting pressure on my stomach wound and I'm now watching as my blood seeps out and trickles onto the stone floor like a grotesque waterfall. I hope I bleed out soon. That would be for the best.

More have come, you see.

Five or six gulls just squeezed through the smashed window one-by-one and are making their way to my bed. One piece of good news, I have my whisky. I just hope it takes the edge off the pain that is to come.

A gull just jumped up onto my bed and I can see its yellow eyes staring into my soul.

ANIMAL UPRISING!

OLD SHUCK
Patrick Winters

1825

❝ It's true enough, I tell you! I saw it myself, just the other night!"

"Bah!" Clarence Smith spat in return, waving off his friend's superstitious assertions. "No, you bloody did not."

"Yes, I did!" Gerald Jones maintained, following after Smith as they strode along the walkway. The din of three dozen running power looms rose up from below them, the constant whirling noise filling the entire cotton mill. Late afternoon light stole its way through the grime-coated windows about them, the dusty air stirring as though it were alive.

"You may very well have seen a black dog," Smith retorted, growing more and more exasperated with his friend, "but you didn't see no Old Shuck!"

"Yes, I did!" Jones repeated, pointing an accusatory finger to the other foreman's back. "I came out of my house the morning 'fore last, in the thick of all that rain we had, and as I made my less-than-merry way onto Silk Street, I looked down an alley, and there it was! A great big dog—the biggest damned hound I ever laid eyes upon—with a shaggy coat of fur that was coal-black. And its eyes were raging red, like the fires of Perdition itself! My ghost nearly left my bones then and there, I'll warrant! Then it was gone, back into the shadows."

Smith shook his head, gazing down at his feet with a smirk as they kept on around the walkway. Jones, however, was far from through.

"And I'm not the only one who's seen it, either! That infernal thing's been sighted all over Manchester these last weeks, and it's a certain omen of death to whoever comes upon it! Just the other day, some tradesman said he saw it before the cathedral, of all places! And that four-legged

22

demon *leapt* upon him, snarling and barking! Not satisfied with letting him die in good time, it seems! And you know what else? The cathedral is only a short way off from where *I* saw the beast on Silk Street!"

"Oh, indeed?" Smith sighed, stopping and turning about to face his friend. "Well, maybe that tradesman had himself a good nip of the bottle that evening, and Old Shuck smelled it on him from all the way down in the underworld; crawled on up to ask the git for a taste of its own!"

Smith gave a chuckle, lifting his hands as a tired mother would before a fitful child. "As a matter of fact, I bet all of these superstitious clods who claim to be seeing devil-dogs about had a good nip or two before their *terrible* encounters! So tell me, Jonesy—and be honest—what did *you* have the morning of yours? A snifter of brandy or a full pint of lager?"

"Laugh now," Jones said, eyes wide and skin pale, "but let's see if you do the same after I'm dead within the month! Try and have a good giggle when you're attending my funeral, why don't you?"

"Oh, 'swounds! Would you—?"

"Gentlemen!"

The scratchy, albeit commanding voice rose up behind them. Its lashing notes were all too familiar to the men, and they stiffened rightly as they turned to face Alastair Harris, owner and overseer of the mill. He stood at their backs, his ashen face glowering, as per usual.

"I neither pay you to waste the day talking of supernatural drivel, nor to block my walkways and bar me from my office." His steely stare shifted between them. "Do I?"

"No, sir," Smith answered, his grin abashed.

"Absolutely not, sir," Jones agreed, his fervor effectively sobered under his employer's gaze.

Harris nodded with finality. "Then desist in both and get back to work."

Smith and Jones slipped aside, allowing their employer to pass between them.

Harris' feet smacked against the walkway as he continued on towards his office, which hung nestled in the dark corner of the mill, looming over all below. He strode with his hands clasped behind his back, peering down his nose to the looms and those who were operating them, a cursory look to ensure that all was running well. Pleased with the work that he saw, he set his sights before him once more and turned his mind to other matters.

As he stepped into the office, his clerk and assistant, Harold Wilkinson, gave him a flustered and forcefully cheery greeting. Harris gave a hushed *harrumph* in return, moving right on towards his own, much larger desk across the room. He sat himself down and set to reading and signing miscellaneous paperwork, analyzing reports of his mill's output, and stewing in a brooding silence that seemed to ill-befit one so wealthy and well-off as he.

Wilkinson, meanwhile, saw to his own humble tasks. He did not dare so much as breathe a breath that was louder than the dull hum of the looms coming from beyond the walls; he moved and worked with the softness of a mouse before a patient trap, maintaining the silence as best as he could.

The staggering stillness was finally broken a quarter hour later, when shouting voices and rushed, clanging footsteps upon the walkways reached their ears.

The office door flung open, with one Samuel Taylor doing the flinging.

The recently sacked worker stood there with a solemn look on his bearded face, his clothes dirtied and the flat cap upon his head bearing a ratty hole.

One of the mill's portly guards came running up behind him, huffing a good deal.

"I'm sorry, sir!" the guard said to Harris, who remained behind his desk, looking at the scene with a calm demeanor; Wilkinson had risen to his feet, surprised at the outburst and ever fidgety. "I tried to stop 'im, but 'e ran right on past me at the post! Quite insistent, 'e seems!"

"Yes, I can see that," Harris said flatly. He set his pen and papers aside and clasped his hands, setting them on his desk, appearing attentive. "Gather your breath, now; you'll need it to see him out in a moment. In the meantime, would you care to explain this intrusion, Mr. Taylor? I seem to recall having released you from the mill not four days ago."

Taylor's sad face fell all the more as he spoke. "Yes, sir; I know, sir. But, please . . . I've come to ask you to reconsider. I need this job. Work is hard to find these days, after all. And I've worked your mill these last two years! Why, I know this place as well as I know my own body! I've given you good work!"

Harris made no motion, nor did his stony visage show the least measure of sympathy as he responded.

"Indeed, you did, Mr. Taylor. And 'did' will remain the optimal word on the matter. You must understand that I—and many others in the business of textiles—appreciate the value of cheap labor. And I and other factory owners are coming to realize the cheapest labor comes from employing younger, spryer souls than you. A child can complete the tasks that you do here, and so one shall. Simple, efficient business, Mr. Taylor."

"But, sir," Taylor implored, stepping closer to Harris and his desk, "I have a family to take care of! They depend upon me and the wages I earn. Matters were difficult enough for us as they were; when I wasn't tending to the looms, I was out of the city, hunting just to put meat on the table! Why, without your employment—"

"You'll have plenty more time to spend in the woods, looking for more meat," Harris cut him off, growing tired of this matter now that he'd had his say. "I wish you luck in the hunt for both game and employment elsewhere."

The guard made to grab Taylor's arm, but Taylor shook it off. His face went from sorrowfully slack to angrily taut; his meek and mild begging became exasperated sighs.

"Sir, I *must* have my job back! I'm desperate. I have children, for God's sake! A boy and a girl, hungry and wanting in a cold home!"

Harris still did not seem moved in the least by the man's pleas. He blinked once, twice, and then spoke in that persisting and maddeningly blunt fashion.

"You are not the first 'desperate' man that I have sacked, Mr. Taylor, and you certainly will not be the last. And while I do not receive any pleasure at terminating your employment, it will not set my heart to breaking, either. So, save your woes and your pleas; they will win you naught here. As for your children: perhaps one of them may qualify for your old job. I suggest you bring the boy in, if you are in such dire straits; we pay the boys a halfpenny more."

Silence settled over the room for a prolonged moment as Samuel Taylor glared at Harris, enraged tears at the corners of his eyes. The tears were the only remaining hint of his sorrow; the rest of him—from his shaking frame to his fiery-red face—spoke of the rage that had taken him as he listened to his former employer's callous words.

"There's a special place in Hell for people like you, Harris," Taylor sneered. "People who use and play with their fellow man, like a dog with a bone."

Harris' stone face finally broke at this insult—and it broke into a small, careless smile. "And I'm sure there's a special place in your Heaven for those who live and die poor." He lifted a hand, motioning to the guard. "Please see Mr. Taylor out now."

The guard grabbed Taylor's elbow again, and this time, Taylor allowed it. He side-stepped along as he was rushed out, and before the guard shut the door behind them, Taylor glared back at Harris and said, "You'll pay for this, you bastard."

"Perhaps," Harris said to the musty air a moment later, "but then, *I* can afford to."

He returned to his papers, going on with his duties as though nothing had interrupted him, let alone vexed him. Wilkinson, who had watched the whole ordeal in mute dismay, sat back down and tried to continue on with his work, in kind, a perturbing knot in his gut. It gave a twist when Harris spoke to him.

"You will have to stay late this evening, Wilkinson. I will need your help in going over and completing textile orders."

"Y— yes, sir, Mr. Harris," Wilkinson stammered.

The clerk went back to his papers, lamenting that he would have to spend an extra hour or two with the ever-demanding, ever-unfeeling Alastair Harris.

And so the hours crept by until the mill closed, its workers shambling homewards as the western sky shined with the last lingering glow of sunset. Harris, Wilkinson, and the lone, portly guard were the only ones left in the factory by the time night had settled in full. It wasn't until the clock was on the verge of striking nine that the three stepped out into the streets, their day finally at an end.

The men bundled up against the slight chill of the evening, the guard and Wilkinson giving Harris their insincere farewells. Harris gave them a half-hearted wave of his hand, turning his back on them as each made their way down a different street and homewards.

26

The sporadic lampposts here and about had been lit and now shone overhead, casting the streets into increments of golden light and cowering shadow, where the light could not fully reach. The sky above was veiled in soupy clouds, the promise of a full moon's glow shining only dimly through and beyond the buildup; there were no stars to speak of in the heavens, nor souls to see across the earth. The streets were quite barren at this hour. Harris' leisurely steps plodded against the cobblestone and through the stillness, echoing off of the gray faces of the looming buildings about him.

He walked on for a few dim blocks, unperturbed and lost to thoughts of business, before the distant knell of the striking hour rang out through the night.

No sooner had the song started than he heard the sound of animalistic growling coming from somewhere in the shadows about him.

Harris slowed to a halt, the noise awakening some caution within him. He gazed ahead and then back the way he had come, seeing no sign of any creature along the street. He listened for the patter of feet, the swish of a tail, or another troubled growl, but all had gone still yet again.

He began to think that he had heard nothing at all, save for some silly whit of his imagination.

Satisfied enough with this, he made to continue on; but before he could even lift his foot for another assured step, the sound of some hound giving a rough clearing of its nose stayed him.

He turned about, looking nervously to the other side of the street, where the great doorway of an office building sat shrouded in the night.

In that moment, the machinations of the universe (or perhaps some darker, smirking force) came into perfect, terrible alignment: as another tolling of the bell sounded out, and as the low growling picked up once more, the clouds overhead began to shift. They slipped from each other— like woven fingers unweaving—just enough to send a shaft of moonlight shooting to the earth, falling upon the threshold of that blackened doorway that held Harris' eye. And in that gradual illumination, he saw the dark form of a great big dog, sitting at attention and looking straight at him.

Harris observed the beast and its menacing presence with a dawning sense of foreboding.

Its obsidian-colored fur held the shimmer of the light, growing thick and wild about its bulky body. Its legs and its haunches looked astonishingly muscular and long, and its head was equally large, ears pointed up and poised like a statue. Dagger-edged teeth poked out of its long maw, its lips turned up in its continuing snarl.

But the most sinister of all its mighty canine attributes, by far, were its eyes. They were narrowed, and they shined with an unnatural scarlet essence, as though fashioned from the very first torrid fires that Hell had ever known. It was quite an impossible thing, and yet there they were, their terrible sights upon Harris—and it chilled his very spirit to know it.

He recalled the argument he'd heard just that afternoon, stuck behind the bantering Clarence Smith and the high-strung Gerald Jones; he remembered his burning irritation and near nausea at hearing talk of "devil-dogs" and the foolish like. But now, with this unholy thing before his very eyes, he was forced to reckon such blatant disregard of otherworldly things. His rational mind was all of a sudden dashed upon the stones of doubt, and he feared that his skin—indeed, his very soul—could now be rent by the teeth of this bizarre creature.

That dread went soaring to new heights as the hound raised its head towards the moon and let loose a call that was caught between a wolf's howl and a phantom's wail.

This awful sound was what finally loosened Harris' knees and set his feet to racing down the street.

He ran faster than he ever had before, caught in a maelstrom of fear. His soles smacked along the cobblestones and his coat billowed out as he made to dash down a side alley. The dark and narrow way became filled with the racket of his steps, his whimpering, and yet another howl from the creature, the baying rising and falling over him like a sea's wave. It pushed him on and out into the next street, then on to the next, and he kept on running until the howling trailed off into silence.

Harris paused, just long enough to listen to the alleys. His ears discerned the scratching of nails upon stones and the ragged breaths of the beast at his back. It was chasing after him.

Harris dashed off again, taking alleyways and streets as they came, not rightly thinking of where he was going; the only thought in his head was the desperate hope of some sanctuary. He cried out as he went, eyes locked ahead, imploring someone to help and shelter him, and begging a God he had never put faith in to save his soul. But the streets remained desolate, all the doors stayed shut, and nary an angel swooped down to lift him on high.

The calamitous noise of growling and the persistent patter of paws filled the night, as though all the hounds of Hell were now racing after him. It was driving him to the edge of his sanity, and eventually, to the edge of the River Irwell.

Heaving his labored breaths, he kept on along a paved path beside the narrow portion of the stretching waterway. A small stone bridge hung just overhead, arching over to the next bank and casting the path into a length of shadow.

As he entered that darkness, Harris' weary legs finally failed him. He gave a cry as he tumbled face-first onto the cold stones. All of his breath left him as his chest hit the ground, his sides erupting with instant pain. The yapping and snarling grew nearer as he struggled to crawl on, tears in his eyes and pleas at his quivering lips. When he felt teeth digging into his calf and dragging him back, his entreaties gave way to his screams.

He heard his trousers rip and felt flesh and muscle tearing away from his leg. As he dug his fingers into the ground—and to his ever-growing surprise—another pair of jaws came gnashing into his wrist; the black devil-dog was not alone.

Harris looked to his bloodied, agony-stricken arm and saw that it was a black and brown German Shepherd that had a hold of his wrist, a collar about its leashed neck; looking back, he saw a Doberman Pinscher—likewise leashed—still tearing at his heel. And worse yet, another one came running up to join its compatriots in the slaughter.

The devil-dog, it turned out, was nowhere in sight. That fact provided him little solace as the three canines unleashed their fury upon him as one, biting and rending his limbs as they sleeked their tongues with his blood. His wails rose all the more as he tried to break free, to no avail.

Those mournful cries had reached Samuel Taylor's ears long before he caught up with his hunting dogs and their grisly kill. The slighted man slowed his run as soon as the bridge came into sight, and he approached the shadowed underpass with gradual, uncertain steps.

This was what he had wanted; this was how he would see his threat to Harris fulfilled.

After Harris' insult, he had returned home, rallying up and leading his hunting dogs through the night for this purpose alone. He had no intention of simply scaring his former employer with their presence; Harris' cold words had seen to that, sending the chill of bloody vengeance into his heart, instead. He had sat with them for hours in the shadow of the mill, just waiting for Harris to leave. When he had, Taylor pushed the dogs on, tracking the businessman through the streets until the opportune moment arose—when Taylor felt he could loose them upon the bastard and let them have their way with him.

"I wish you luck in the hunt." Taylor had laughed at Harris' own words, for luck was just what they'd had in slinking quietly through the streets, keeping their presence at his back unknown. They had fallen no more than a block behind him all the while. However, after some other dog's wild howl had risen up through the streets, his own dogs' orneriness could not be contained any longer. At that moment, they had pulled against their leashes with such force that they slipped from Taylor's grip. They went on after Harris of their own accord, snarling and bolting off like rabid beasts with the scent of blood. Taylor chased after them as they tracked down Harris, and now, here they all were.

His revenge upon his former employer had come to pass; but as much as he had yearned for it, to see it meted out . . .

It was far more terrible than he could have imagined. He watched the silhouettes of his dogs pulling apart the shadow that was Alastair Harris with a mixture of both vindication and revulsion.

The *sounds* . . .

That *screaming* . . .

His stomach gave a lurch as Harris' yells started to grow weak and ragged. He turned away from the scene, his whole body caught between rage and disgust and shaking with their conflict. He looked to the river for a moment, and then back down the path trailing beside it.

He froze as he caught sight of a great black dog sitting alert in the middle of the path. Its eyes of burning red stared at him through the darkness.

He kept his eyes fast upon it, until Harris' grunts had turned to whimpers, and then stopped altogether. His dogs came stepping up to him a moment later, their noses wet and red and leashes scraping the ground. They sat at his side, bowing their heads and whining lightly as they, too, noticed the curiously large hound.

A moment crept by as Taylor and the beast continued observing one another. Then, the dog rose, turned about, and returned to wherever it had come from, dashing off into the night.

Swallowing down the lump in his throat, Taylor snatched up his dogs' leashes. He led them over to the river's edge, where he knelt and cupped his hands in the water, pouring it onto the snout of each dog, washing away the blood. After the quick cleaning, he rushed them along and homewards. He refused to look back at the shadow-covered scraps of what was once Alastair Harris.

Harris' body would be discovered the following day, its terrible state sparking further rumors and fears of Old Shuck making its rounds about the city, dispensing death in the wake of its appearance.

A week later, Samuel Taylor died quite unexpectedly, having been trampled after a team of spooked horses brought their hooves and their carriage bearing down upon him in the streets. None who witnessed the tragedy could explain what had terrified and stirred the horses into such action.

Another week later, the superstitious Gerald Jones succumbed to a sudden and nasty affliction of the flu that had brought him low days before. His friend, Clarence Smith, did not laugh in the least when attending his funeral.

HOW DOES YOUR GARDEN GROW
M. R. Deluca

"COME AROUND BACK. IN THE GARDEN" the hand-scrawled sign read.

The reporter obliged, stepping off the porch and ambling around the modest but proudly-kept split-level home. He noticed that every set of windows had the curtains pulled tight, probably in a vain attempt to keep out the blazing summer sun.

Wyoming weather was fickle at best, and the temperature could be downright punitive, especially in the rural parts. The bipedal inhabitants were often at least a fifteen minutes' worth drive from one another; these people were no exception, their house the only one dotting miles and miles of ranching property. Yes, only the people with a real, physical connection to the land stayed here for long.

The reporter turned the corner to see a backyard with the most beautiful garden he had ever seen. Common flowers, rare flowers, lush shrubs, all of them thick, spilled over in an artful kaleidoscope that rivaled many professional botanical gardens. The explosion of color growing in soil this close to the Rockies was both unusual and impressive. Little wonder his editor sent him to cover the story. Whatever this lady fed her plants, it worked wonders.

A woman with tawny-colored hair and a thin strip of silver down her part sensed the extra presence; she looked up from where she kneeled among the hydrangeas, and tightly smiled at the man. She rubbed her gloved hands together to shake the excess dirt and extended a still-clothed hand from where she sat. "Mr. Willoughby, I presume."

He took it as a cue that she wasn't moving for anything or anyone. It seemed unsurprising she liked her plants more than people; these meticulous enthusiasts all too often preferred honing their craft to exchanging niceties with strangers. Fine. He would go to her.

He took her hand. "Please, call me Lyle." He knew she gardened—it was the whole reason he was there—but still didn't expect the slight woman's grip to be so firm.

He didn't bother wiping away any excess dirt on his hand—she would probably take it as an insult to her garden, or something like that. "So, Mrs. Tucker—"

"Call me Daisy. I'm not that much older than you, so there's no need to address me like I'm some matronly figure." She sounded irked. The interview was getting off to a great start already.

"All right, Daisy," Lyle said as charmingly as he could. He extracted a pad and pen from his messenger bag and posed, ready to write. "So how does it feel winning the Rockies regional division of the Grow Your Garden Championship, three years running?"

She half smiled. "It doesn't feel bad, I'll tell you that."

She was not going to make this easy. "Good, good. It's impressive," he prompted. "Very few gardeners ever even place in a contest as big as this, but to win not once, not twice, but thrice in a row?" He let out a low whistle. "You haven't just got a green thumb, you must have a whole green hand."

"I guess I do."

"I did some digging of my own—just a bit of journalist-gardener crossover humor." He grinned, but the corners of her mouth didn't even twitch. "Some of these plants wouldn't fare in such rocky soil or such fluctuating temperatures and humidity. What's your secret?"

"If I told you, it wouldn't be a secret anymore."

She didn't like him asking all these questions. He reminded her of the type who would expose his own mama's deepest, darkest secrets if he could score a front page article in a major coastal paper.

Lyle Willoughby looked like a man in the middle. He was of middle height, middle weight, and from a mid-sized paper in a mid-sized city in, well, the middle of the country. Even the handshake he gave her was of average strength. The only metric by which he was extreme, was his ambition.

33

Lyle had started out on the bottom. His parents died in a plane crash when he was too old to get adopted, so he became a "hot potato" foster kid, tossed from home to home and, occasionally, living on the streets (which was sometimes preferable to some of the foster families). It made his resolve steely and his heart colder than he would ever like to admit. But it got him to where he was today, and for that he was grateful.

Broke and alone as a teenager, he hadn't the money for a place to live, let alone attend college; so, he hustled his way into an entry-level position in a small newspaper as soon as he acquired working papers, and went to high school at night. Having responsibility for only himself and no real connection to anyone else allowed him to throw himself into his work and climb that career ladder. Right now he was on a comfortable, middle rung, but hoped that saying yes to all of the smaller, unimportant assignments that crossed his path would better his chance of making it at a newspaper that was actually read by people outside the immediate region.

She looked at the large-faced watch on her wrist. "Nice of you to stop by. It's going to be dark soon. Safe trip back." She tended to a patch of bright, almost tropical-looking flowers.

He wanted to hightail it just as much as she wanted him to, if not more, but he needed more quotes for his article. He couldn't come home empty-handed, and her curt quips wouldn't cut it in the lifestyle section of a major regional paper. He wasn't going to let some cranky woman make him look bad in front of his boss.

"Just a few more questions, Daisy, and I'll be out of your hair." She was too young to be so crotchety: she could be a young grandmother, at the oldest. "Just out of curiosity, do you have many visitors around these parts?"

"Barely anyone comes out here. The garden judges were here last month, and a photographer from your paper was here a few days ago. But honestly, some weeks the only person who comes around is the mail carrier."

How surprising, given her warm, inviting demeanor. "So you live alone?"

Her eyes lit up. "Oh, no. My husband Douglas is out herding cattle, and my two grandkids are upstairs."

"Really." Maybe he could make this more of a family interest piece, since she was so averse to talking about her garden. "Do they help you plant? Maybe we can go in the house and I could talk to them—"

Daisy returned to her earlier, irritated expression. "Look, I understand these interviews are obligatory and all, but if we're being honest, neither of us wants to be out here in this heat making trivial small talk. My grandkids in there, they're young, and I've left them alone long enough already. Excuse me if I seem rude, but I must get back to them. If you have any more questions, you have my permission to make up something that sounds okay. Happy trails." She gathered her tools, gave a dismissive nod, and started toward the house. Lyle followed.

"Daisy, wait," he called as she opened the back door. "Are you sure we can't finish our discussion in the house? It'll be five more minutes, tops." He could also really use five minutes in the air conditioning and a drink of water.

She shook her head. "I don't let strange men in the house with my grandkids. Sorry, but the answer is no." She shut the door and he heard the lock click almost immediately.

Lyle shoved his pad and pen away and stormed to his car in front of the house. When they had spoken on the phone, Daisy was friendly, charming even; that is, until he brought up an in-person interview at her house. She had declined, and then begrudgingly acquiesced when he mentioned his paper had bought special rights that year for an exclusive spread on the three-year winner, and that it was simple: no interview, no five figure prize money. He thought she was just upset about having to tidy up her house, or something like that, but she didn't let him even see the inside. He just stood in the garden, with no chair, no fan, no water, and only a pathetic, short transcript to show for the time, travel, and expense of trekking out to no man's land.

He opened the car door and paused. He didn't get to where he was by backing down from a challenge. And he wasn't going to get to where he wanted by retreating and admitting to his editor that he failed. He was going to get his interview, whether she liked it or not.

He marched back up to the door and knocked. There was no answer, but there was rhythmic thudding from inside the house. He moved off the step and to the closest window.

Lyle peered in, hoping the curtains would move eventually. They were thick and opaque, and—success. They finally parted enough for him to catch a glimpse of just what she was hiding in that house.

And what a glimpse he caught: a little brown-haired boy bounding down a set of stairs into a living room, yelling "Pokey, wait for me!" at a horned rabbit running in circles on the living room rug.

Lyle stepped back and blinked rapidly, adjusting his eyes. The sun might have been messing with his vision, likely a result of prolonged exposure from being in the garden so long. He had to take another look.

When the curtains opened again, he got another look at Pokey. Pokey raced up the steps, with the boy hot on his heels. A little girl waiting at the top of the stairs scooped up the rabbit into a big hug, expertly avoiding its knife-like antlers. The kids were smiling, obviously not in any danger.

His heart thumped in his chest, his adrenaline kicking. Pokey was a jackalope: a real, live jackalope.

During his youth, the library was his favorite place to be because the foster homes he was living in weren't. It was really the only home he had, a safe, dependable, and comfortable getaway from the rest of his problems. He read anything and everything he could get a hold of, on just about every subject known to man. Cryptozoology, the pseudoscience of scientifically unverified animals, happened to be one of those subjects.

He had read all about jackalopes; he remembered being intrigued at the Western mythical beast. Jackalopes were jackrabbits with sharp antelope antlers, fast critters with a hankering for whiskey. They could be found in places like Wyoming, where they mimicked cowboys' singing and confused hunters with their imitative human voice. They spawned only during lightning storms, couldn't pierce stovepipes, and, with the appropriate permit, could be hunted on June 31st.

If he wasn't hallucinating right now, then this wasn't cryptozoology; this crossed over into plain old zoology.

He returned to his truck and grabbed his camera and the whiskey he occasionally used for himself as a pick-me-up. He had refilled it right before the trip, thinking he would need it. He was right—just not in the way he thought. As he stuffed the flask in an inside pocket, he heard a little boy sing an old Western song, and then a noticeably older-sounding tenor copy him.

But there was no grown man in the house. Daisy had said so herself, if she wasn't lying.

Oh, yes. He wasn't crazy. But he was going to have to take a picture to prove it.

He knocked on the door again. No one answered, he realized, because he couldn't be heard over the singing and thudding. He then banged hard with a clenched fist and yelled out, "Daisy Tucker! It's an emergency!"

He could see the front headline: "Where the Deer and the Jackalope Play." His story would sound worthy of trashy tabloid, but really be reporting on the fringes of unexplored science. This was it. This was his ticket to the big leagues.

A couple minutes later, Daisy opened the door a smidge. "What's the matter?" she asked, first concerned and then leery when she noticed his car wasn't steaming.

"I saw your rabbit in there." He couldn't help the smug smile spreading across his face. She thought she could pull the wool over his eyes; but he was too smart for that.

Her eyes narrowed suspiciously. "How do you know I have a rabbit?"

"When you didn't answer the door, I peeked through your window. The AC—" which spout nice, cool air that he faintly felt from the doorway—"lifted the curtain slightly and I saw your presumed grandson playing with an odd-looking creature he called Pokey."

"Now you're spying on us?"

What did she expect him to do? Making up an interview was below his journalistic integrity. "I want to see Pokey, and I'm not leaving until I do."

"I don't understand all the fuss. Do other folks have a stranger show up on their doorstep, demanding to see their pet bunny? It's downright indecent. And harassing."

This was not the type of person she wanted on her porch, or anywhere near her grandkids. It's a good thing she sent them upstairs to play with Pokey while she dealt with this big city snake.

Now if she could just get him to slither back home.

"Daisy, that was no ordinary bunny I saw. That was a jackalope." This was his foot in the door to one of those pretentious papers on the coasts, and the both of them knew it.

"Actually, it's a rabbit with that virus—papilloma, I think. That's why it has horns. Now good day." She started to shut the door.

He jammed his foot in the doorway.

"Get away from my family!" She shoved back hard, almost throwing him backwards.

He caught his balance and threw his full weight against the door.

"I'm not after your family." He angrily gritted his teeth. "You've got the most mythical creature in the West in your house, and I'm not leaving until I get a picture."

A struggle ensued, but it was over in less than a minute when Lyle overpowered her and stormed into the house. He was in the living room and heading for the stairs.

She grabbed the back of his jacket and a flask flew out of an inside pocket. The metal tin hit the carpet and the cap flew off, allowing the contents to leak out.

In an instant a brown blur flew down the stairs. Lyle's mouth hung open in shock. But not because he finally saw the jackalope up close and personal. It was because it had gored its horns clean through his legs, piercing the shin bones with a sickening crunch.

He swayed, struggling to keep his balance.

Daisy screamed and ran into the kitchen to get a dishtowel to slow the hemorrhaging.

But it was too late. She returned just as Lyle Willoughby finally collapsed, pitching forward. Pokey charged once again. It hit Lyle again with its antlers, this time square in the chest, where his heart was— or should have been.

The jackalope squirmed out from under the deadweight of the intruder and, self-satisfied, hopped on over to the delicious whiskey spilt nearby. Quick as a flash, it was lapping up the drink and twitching its whiskers like the happy drunk bunny it was.

"Bad Pokey!" she scolded as she marched over and scooped up the flask. "We do not use our horns to impale people. Go back upstairs!"

The furry bunny beast looked up, its eyes big and innocent like a cottontail's, and hiccupped. It flashed a shy yet sly smile and woozily hopped upstairs, crooning that melancholic old miners' song, "You are lost and gone forever, dreadful sorry..." At one point it stumbled into the wall and skewered the plasterboard before moseying on over to the kids' room for a cuddle and a nap.

She clenched her hands and then unclenched them. Never mind the stairs. She had more important things to deal with at that moment. Like the really dead guy in her living room.

Daisy marched outside to find a familiar truck heading to her house. She breathed a sigh of relief.

"You're back early," she said when she reached the top of the driveway.

Douglas kissed her hello. "Those cows must have been starving, because they ate so quickly the time went by in a flash."

"Speaking of a flash—"

He grew solemn and cocked an eyebrow. "Pokey?"

"Yup."

"What happened?"

"That reporter from that metro paper a few states over, the one who came over to do a piece on my award-winning garden, discovered Pokey."

"Oh boy."

"He gored him in the living room. It was absolutely bloody." She grimaced at the recollection. "The man's still leaking from all those holes Pokey put in him."

"What a beast." He clicked his tongue. "Poor Wyatt and Cynthia. They've had that bunny since they were little babies. They've already had their parents taken away from them. He was going to take away their beloved pet, too, and any sense of normality they have." He shuddered. He and Daisy lost their daughter in that lightning storm three years ago, and the memory itself might have faded, but the emotion behind it never did.

"Now the paper's going to send some investigators over here, have some shiny-shoed detectives sniff around and ask questions." He thought for a minute. "Maybe you should have let him unmask Pokey. We wouldn't have this problem. Pokey would be locked up in a government cage for testing. The kids would be crushed, but maybe they shouldn't have such an oddball pet that they have to hide from the world."

Daisy steeled her eyes. "Remember when you went out looking for Jessie and Zeke when they didn't get back from riding? Douglas, you finding that baby jackalope near their horses was a sign. I still believe that.

They were struck by lightning, and that bunny was sitting there, all helpless and shivering right next to them. Life was born when life was taken away." She swallowed the lump in her throat. "I honestly believe their mother's spirit now lives in that rabbit, one way or another, and that's why they're so attached to the thing. That's going to be the only connection to Jessie they're ever going to remember, whether they eventually realize it or not. So I'm keeping that rabbit until the day I die."

"I guess you're right." He cracked his knuckles and looked at the small sedan. "I'll disassemble his car and burn his stuff later. You keep the kids inside. We'll make sure every trace of his ever being here is gone."

"Right," she said as she headed to the house. "I'll clean the living room. Shovel's out back, where it always is."

Douglas grabbed the shovel from the tool shed, and thought to himself about how many holes he dug thanks to Pokey. In a few years, he'll be too old for digging. His back was twinging all the more every day. Oh well. That was a matter he'd have to address when it finally arose. By then, maybe Wyatt would be old enough to take over for him.

Douglas picked a spot on the perimeter of the garden and called out to Daisy, "Is here good?"

She opened the back door and peered out. "Nope, that's taken." She had the better memory of the two, and knew the garden better than the back of her own hand.

"How about here?"

"Just a little left." He obliged. "Perfect."

And so he dug and dug until he had cleared a hole long enough and deep enough for that reporter. He shook his head. All these nosy people just made their lives harder. Then he went inside to fetch the body, and with a little struggle, lugged and deposited it in the makeshift grave.

He saw the O frozen on Lyle's lifeless face. "Poor guy. Now he's flower food," he thought.

Douglas filled up the hole and called out as he approached the kitchen, "All right, I put him with the rest."

And so lay Lyle Willoughby for eternity, along with seventeen of his other busybody comrades, encircling the prettiest garden in the Rockies— the only garden ever improved by a rabbit.

THE DAY OF THE DEER FLIES
Stanley B. Webb

D awn!
What a glorious moment to start my day hike into the Adirondack Mountains. The mosquitoes had retired to their shadowy homes, and the daytime pests had not yet emerged.

The black fly had a reputation as the worst pest in the Northeast wilderness. In the springtime they arise in swarms thick enough, so it is said, to drive cattle insane.

By the Fourth of July, the black flies had died off.

However, the black fly is not the worst.

Deer flies had come into season. They are as big as blow flies, and they like to swarm around your head and burrow under your hair to drill for blood in your scalp. I hated them, but the beauty of the Adirondacks made them endurable.

I parked my car near a trailhead in the village of Wanakena, and left the doors unlocked, for there was nothing worth stealing except my spare gasoline, which I kept locked in the trunk.

I shouldered a small pack, which contained a few bottles of water and a sandwich, and hung my binoculars around my neck. I carried a book of matches as well. I planned to do no cooking, but if I became lost I would need a fire. I signed the trailhead logbook, then stepped around the old steel car gate.

The trail used to be a fire access road, until Article 14 of the New York Constitution, also known as the "forever wild" law, had prohibited all motor vehicles from entering the Forest Preserve.

My hike started through a marsh where dead, gray trees loomed over misty pools of filmed water. The trail ascended to firmer ground, and spruce woods closed in around me. The sun rose behind the trees, casting its orange blaze through the green boughs.

A figure approached from up the trail, a bearded young park ranger with an enormous backpack.

He paused to greet me. "Where are you heading?"

"Cat Mountain, just for the day."

"I hope you signed in," he said. "That helps us find you in an emergency."

"I did."

"Good, I hope you enjoy yourself."

He went on toward Wanakena. I continued into the park.

Suddenly an animal burst out of the woods. I jumped back with a fearful shout, thinking at first that it was a bear, but it was just a deer. The deer skidded to a stop, its eyes rolling in panic, then it plunged back into the woods. I laughed with relief. Apparently the deer had been asleep beside the trail, and my approach had frightened it awake.

I continued on my way.

The morning's first deer fly arrived, and went into orbit around my head. I grabbed at the pest, but missed. I waited until I felt it land on my hair, then seized it. I brought my fist down, and carefully pinched the fly between two fingers. It was an attractive insect. Its body and wings were yellow with bands of brown. Its eyes were striped with green and gold.

Its mouthpart was a black spike.

Deer flies are hard to crush. You cannot roll one to death in your fingers, as you can a mosquito. I pulled the fly's head off, and tossed its body to the ground. The deerfly's wings buzzed, and its decapitated body spun.

I spent a moment to pity the animals. Evolution had favored the human species. Animals had no hands with which to deal with biting pests. The best that they could do was to twitch their skins, or slap with their tails. I could believe that an animal might go mad in a swarm of deer flies.

More deer flies came, to circle my head as electrons circle an atomic nucleus. I waved and slapped to keep them off my scalp, but one of them struck lower and pierced the back of my neck. I pinched the fly off my skin and beheaded it.

Fatigue suddenly overcame me. I thought that I was tired because I had risen earlier than usual, to reach the mountains before dawn. I slipped my pack off and sat down on a rock beside the trail. I took a bottle of water from one of the pack's side pockets and raised it to my mouth.

My fingers trembled. The bottle fell to the ground. I bent to pick it up. My hand would not close properly, and the bottle slipped again. The tremors spread up my arm. I attempted to raise my hand and found that I lacked the strength.

All of my limbs began to tremble. A feeling of pins-and-needles spread on my extremities. I panicked and tried to get up, but only rose a few inches before collapsing. My arms would not move to break my fall. I turned my face aside before landing prone on the trail. My binoculars bruised my chest.

The pins-and-needles sensation faded away and I lay paralyzed.

My body had become an inert mass, which defied my panicked attempt to move. I tried to understand what was happening to me. Perhaps my diner breakfast had been tainted, or I might have contracted a new disease, or been born with an unsuspected genetic disorder which had now struck.

I suffered the terrifying thought that the paralysis would reach my lungs, or my heart. But, then something equally terrible happened.

The deer flies swarmed on me and fed. They bit my face and hands. Some of them became entangled in my hair, where they buzzed helplessly. Their mouthparts penetrated my shirt and socks. Only my blue jeans thwarted them. When they had drunk their fill, others took their places.

From the corner of one eye I glimpsed their waiting swarm above me, like a living cloud of smoke. I could not move my eyes, or even blink. My tears flowed copiously, soothing my dry vision, and blurring the world.

When insects bite, they inject enzymes to prevent their prey's blood from clotting. Those enzymes cause itching. My itching grew and spread, as if it were a fire consuming my skin, and I could not even twitch my finger. I could not even scream.

I attempted to reassure myself. Whatever had happened to me, I was not really alone. This was a holiday weekend, so it would not be long before other hikers discovered me. At the worst, I would have to wait until the ranger came to find me. Thank God that I had signed the log book on my way in.

The deer flies kept feeding.

I hated them.

I wished that they would all die.

I noticed then how still the woods had become. No birds sang, and no chipmunks rustled in the leaves. There was no sound except the wind in the trees and the humming of the deer flies. The silence was ominous. There might be a big animal nearby, scaring all of the smaller animals away.

There might be a bear in the woods.

Suddenly I felt certain that a hungry bear stalked my helpless body. I believed that I heard its padded footsteps creeping nearer, but I could not move to look.

I panicked again, a motionless panic which left me emotionally exhausted.

No bear came.

My view had landed on the trail back to Wanakena. The spruce woods were thickest on one side of the path, the other side less wooded because of the marsh. The sun was still rising, and it moved long shadows westward across the trail. I watched while the shadows withdrew to their sources. The sky turned from morning grey to bright blue. The sun's light crept over my upturned cheek and burned my skin. The fly bites became agony.

I endured it. I could do nothing else.

The woods remained quiet, and no other hikers appeared. I began to wonder if my paralysis was merely a small part of a general calamity. Perhaps there had been an accident at the nearby army base, which resulted in the release of a chemical weapon. Everyone could be lying helpless while the deer flies ate them.

Perhaps nobody would ever come and help me.

I had given up prayer when I was a teenager. I used to laugh at my mother's faith, telling her that religion was a scam to support the clergy.

I prayed that day, as the shadows leaned slowly around the compass of the woods.

The sun set beyond my view. The sky became dusky gray. I felt the chill of evening.

The deer flies retired with the sun.

My burning itch gradually dulled.

The evening darkened. I still hoped that someone would come, that I would see a flashlight beam in the darkness.

The evening became the night.

No one came.

I could still see the trail and the woods, but they were shadows without definition. When the wind blew, the trees looked like monsters.

A veil of shadow lifted from the marsh. The shadow hovered over the path, then floated toward me, whispering. I thought that it was a ghost, or something worse. I thought that it was the Angel of Death coming for me. As it neared, the whispering became a hum. The shadow resolved into millions of airborne motes. I realized then what it really was.

It was a swarm of mosquitoes.

The swarm settled upon my face and hands. Thousands of tiny bites pierced through my shirt. They infiltrated into my clothes, and entered my ears, caressed my dry lips, and crawled into my mouth. Their bite enzymes renewed my itch.

In spite of my suffering, and with my eyes trapped open, I entered a daze that was a semblance of sleep.

I roused when I saw that dawn was coming. Dawn was the perfect time in the mountains. The mosquitoes were gone, and the deer flies were not yet out. I prayed in thanks for the relief.

Pins-and-needles tickled my digits. The sensation crept up my limbs. My fingers began to tremble. The symptoms that I had experienced at the onset of my paralysis were reversing. My body was returning to me! I felt a joy as fierce as my previous fear. I tried to close my hand, and my fingers obeyed me.

My laughter broke the silence.

I was able to stand by sunrise. Most of my body, including my tongue, was covered with scabby fly bites. I spat out a wad of saliva-drowned insects. Dead deerflies were knotted into my hair. I was clumsy, but I grabbed my pack and started back toward the trailhead.

Never before had I felt such joy.

I was hungry and dehydrated. I drained a bottle of water, then ate my sandwich.

I found a mummified red squirrel on the trail. I paused over the dead animal, which had not been there the previous day. Its skin was sucked in to its bones.

Something had drained it.

A deer fly began to orbit me.

I suffered an epiphany.

My overnight paralysis was not an illness or a military accident; it was caused by the bite of a deer fly. An evolutionary event had occurred. The parasites' bite enzymes had mutated into a venom that renders their prey helpless. The red squirrel had been paralyzed, and the pests had sucked it dry.

Other deer flies joined the first one.

I might be mummified by the next morning.

I bolted, swatting at the pests. More deer flies swarmed in, until their numbers blotted out my view of the trail. One of them landed undetected on my cheek and bit me. I swatted the thing hard, and smeared it across my face. My legs turned watery with fear.

I tried to control my panic. I knew that I could not reach my car before I collapsed. I had to take measures to protect myself. I found a comfortable place to sit down.

My hands had begun to tremble.

I drank another bottle of water, and then put my head inside my pack.

Pins-and-needles spread up my limbs.

With my last strength, I pushed my hands into my pants pockets.

After that, I was helpless.

My breathing echoed in the confines of my backpack. Two more bottles of water lay against my cheek. My air soon became stale, but the deer flies had not yet found their way inside.

I hoped that I would not smother on my own bad air.

The pests bit me through my shirt, wherever the fabric touched my skin. I reassured myself that I was too large for them to drain. Still, I had to escape the trail the next morning. I had not had enough fluids to sustain such blood loss for a third night.

I could pass the time best by sleeping. I was fatigued from my ordeal. Even with the deer flies stabbing me through my shirt, I soon began to drift off.

That was when the deer flies found their way into my pack. One by one they crawled inside, but they did not bite. They only crawled around, in search of a way out.

One of them entered my ear, and became trapped. The deer fly buzzed frantically inside my head.

I prayed for God to make it end, but it did not end.

My stomach chortled as my hasty meal worked its way through my system. I helplessly fouled myself.

The light eventually dimmed. The deer flies retreated for the day. My relief was so great that I fell asleep at once.

I awakened to the humming of the mosquitoes. They were biting me through my shirt. They were inside my pack, hovering around my head, waiting for their turn on my face.

Mosquitoes did bite when inside.

I prayed that I would survive until dawn.

I lay in a daze, neither awake nor asleep, when the pins-and-needles returned to my extremities. I tried to move my hand, and failed. My recovery was taking longer than it had the day before. The venom was lingering in my blood.

If I could not move before the deer flies returned, I would never move again.

The light from outside was brighter.

I was sure that I could hear the deer flies coming.

I tried to lift my arm. The limb rose an inch, then fell back. I tried again. My heart pounded with my effort. I reached up to my pack and dragged it off my head.

The orange blaze of sunrise filled the woods.

I hooked my pack over my elbow, then rose to my feet, but fell prone again. I crawled to the trail and dragged myself toward Wanakena. I rose again, and this time stayed up. My coordination was poor. I staggered from one side of the trail to the other, braced myself against trees and boulders, and pushed myself on. Soon, I was able to stay on my feet without support. I stumbled into a half-run.

I heard the deer flies humming in the woods all around me. One of them went into a tight orbit around my head. I grabbed at it, but missed.

The fly landed on my cheek. I slapped it off before it could bite, without pausing to decapitate it.

An opaque swarm surrounded me. I must have drawn all of the deer flies from miles around. I screamed in terror. My fear gave me an adrenaline rush, and I put on more speed. I left the swarm behind for a moment. Glancing back, I saw the huge and furry blob in pursuit.

I passed through the marsh near the trailhead. I saw the ranger whom I had spoken with on the first morning. He lay face down in the mud, and his heavy pack had pushed his head under. Only his legs were visible. Blow flies covered him.

I could see the trail's gate ahead, and my car beyond it.

At the same moment, I felt a bite on my scalp. I reached up, and crushed the deer fly.

"You can't stop me!" I screamed in defiance. "I'm too close, too close!"

I felt pins-and-needles in my fingers. The deer fly's venom was taking effect too fast. I tried to gain speed, but my limbs were cramped from two days of paralysis.

Another fly bit me.

I slammed against the passenger side of my car, and yanked the door open. My legs failed me. I fell across the threshold of the passenger door. I used the seatbelt to drag myself inside.

The swarm darkened the doorway.

I pulled my legs up, stretched out one shaking foot, hooked the toe of my shoe over the door handle, and gave a jerk. The door swung in, and half-latched.

My paralysis became complete.

I expected the flies to swarm in through the improperly closed door.

They only hovered around outside the car. Their massed bodies scraped against the windows. They could not get in.

Then, I saw three deer flies crawling on the inside of the windshield. I waited for them to attack me. They ignored me, and continued crawling on the glass, looking for a way out. With only two bites, my paralysis passed in half an hour.

I closed the door firmly.

I killed the three flies.

I drank my water.

I was a mess. I took off my clothes and cleaned myself as best I could. I had no towels or spare clothing, so I used my backpack. When I was finished, I wanted to throw the stinking thing outside. I reached for the door, but then I quailed.

There was no reason to be afraid. The deer flies had abandoned my car. If they could not smell me, they would not gather. I steeled myself, threw my fouled pack outside, and slammed the door.

I would not allow myself to become afraid to go outside.

I fell deeply asleep.

When I awoke, dawn was near. I started my car and drove to the nearest house. I saw nobody at first, but there was an empty hamper lying in the backyard, with a long pile of laundry nearby. I honked my horn. I reasoned that if the resident had escaped paralysis, then he or she would be hiding indoors. I waited in vain for a face to appear at any of the house's windows.

Then, I noticed a bright gleam among the spilled laundry. I focused my binoculars and discerned a pair of glasses sitting on a blanched nose. What I had perceived as laundry was actually the body of an old woman.

I braced my nerves and opened my door. I ran over to the woman and touched her forehead. She was cold with the morning dew. I returned to my car.

I slowly drove through Wanakena, honking all the while. Nobody responded. I wondered if the deer flies could really have gotten everybody. I decided that they could have. Wanakena was a tiny village, in the middle of our nation's largest state park. The outdoors was the residents' livelihood. Everybody would have gone outside, and nobody would have comprehended the danger.

This was more than an evolutionary event.

This was a war.

I turned on my car radio and picked up a station from the town of Gouverneur, which was about fifty miles away.

If the flies had not spread beyond the Wanakena area, I had a chance to fight back.

I returned to the trailhead and rammed through the rusted old car gate. I drove slowly up the old fire road. My car's springs squealed, and its undercarriage scraped the ground. I drove in to the point where I had first been paralyzed, then I backed and filled until my car pointed back the way I had come.

The sun had not yet risen.

I took my gasoline can out of my trunk and poured all of the fuel out on the forest litter. I stepped back, threw down a match, and returned to my car.

The match's flame spread slowly in the humus, until it met a gasoline fume, and exploded with a thud.

I drove back to the trailhead.

Orange light blazed through the trees.

Smoke obscured the sunrise.

UPSWEEP
Rebecca Gransden

The wail from the deep was ceaseless. For months an array of hydrophones sending signals from the bottom had relayed the presence of the unearthly sound. The noise fluctuated in strength, reaching its peak in the spring before subsiding over the summer. Now, as autumn approached, the mournful groan from the dark depths was rising again.

The sea surface fluttered in black and silver, sparkling in the cold light beams shining out from the research vessel. Marian leant against the railing and gazed into the water, dreading her trip downwards.

A submersible attached to a rival research team had disappeared a few days before, directly beneath where Marian's vessel now gently bobbed in the dark. Her group, being better funded than most, had been called on to head the search. Yo Takagi, the head of the expedition, would want to recover the submersible and the man inside, Peter Meier, before any additional teams even arrived. It was possible, though unlikely, that Meier was still alive.

All communications with the submersible had ended simultaneously, indicating that it had been hit with some sort of shockwave, or suffered catastrophic implosion or crushing. She couldn't refuse the job; she was already on probation having missed the previous expedition due to drinking too much, sleeping in, and forcing her colleagues to leave without her. If she wanted to pursue her studies, she needed to redeem herself.

She stroked the tight-fitting suit, a prototype that had so far been 100% successful on its two previous expeditions. The technology had been tested to destruction in the contained environment of the research facility, but out in the exposure of the open sea she feared unforeseen factors they hadn't prepared for. A protective force field designed to withstand the pressures of the deep sea was generated like a second skin over the exterior surface of the suit, and could only be broken by a signal directed from the vessel. She padded her hands over the suit trying to reassure herself that the closeness she felt was indicative of its protection.

Upsweep, the noise from the deep, squealed and shrieked, singing out from the small front cabin as Takagi turned up the volume of the signal received from below. The sound rushed along the vessel and crept into Marian's torso, its low frequencies a processed version of what she would encounter overboard.

The illuminated cable that would deliver her below swung lightly from its rigging in response to the movement of the boat. Further into the water she watched it descend to the depths, shining white and serpentine, eventually disappearing into the black. She made a final check of herself and looked out to sea at the shadowy waves undulating against the horizon.

The recorded sound of upsweep stopped abruptly and Takagi emerged from the cabin. Without words he initiated the tethering procedure and Marian stepped from the side of the vessel to hang loosely from the brightly glowing cable. The sea was black and still beneath her, lightly chopping against the boat, her legs dangling alongside the thick link to the bottom. The suit had been designed to mimic the gill function of undersea animals and would sustain her for a theoretically indefinite length of time once she was submerged. Takagi gave her an encouraging nod and she furled her body around the cable, the insulating field generated by her suit also engineered to draw her in and fix her in place, ready for the journey downwards.

It would take over an hour to lower her to the spot where contact with the submersible had been lost. To limit the stress of the dive she would enter a form of induced rest, her body held in stasis for the descent into the deep. Takagi tapped final instructions into his tablet and the glowing cable began to unwind. Slowly she entered the icy water, her temperature equalised underneath the responsive barrier of her suit.

She entered the water and was quickly under, buffeted by the swirls and pressures of the surface. These soon dissipated until the smoothness of the restful undersea currents took over, the glide downwards silent and sedate. Marian moved her body into position, her arms and legs coiling around the cable, and, bowing her head, succumbed to programmed half-sleep for her trip to the bottom.

The flow of water roused her in the dark. It travelled from the gloom and whooshed around her skull, as if she'd been woken from a dream by the tidal wake of a large creature. The light of the cable overwhelmed the blackness and she felt the insignificance of her tiny frame adrift in a watery underworld. She blinked herself awake and disentangled her body from the attraction of the cable. The suit, responsive to her movements, propelled her away from her link to the surface. She drifted out into the black, down further, towards the last known location of the submersible.

Vast bubble fields, lit up from below by the shifting of fresh lava flows, jetted from seabed valleys and fissures in the distance. Directly below her, monolithic towers of black volcanic rock jutted from the ocean floor, a city of craggy high-rises. She homed in on a particular black column as a flash of light came from one of the many crevices that defined their construction. As she neared it a blast impacted her and sent her tumbling backwards into the void of open water. The suit stabilised her before her mind could catch up and she struggled to contain her breathing. She turned and, recovering her blurry vision, refocused on the source of the flash. All was dark in the crevice but she squinted and could make out a domed outline, at odds with the sharp character of the rock formation. She turned off her own illumination and, with nothing more than the residue of the light from the surface and the soft glow from the cable lulling in the water behind her, she set off once more towards the dark underwater tower.

This time she veered around and approached from an angle that sent her on a less direct advance. She reached the tower and took a moment to rest. The sound of upsweep curled around the towers, brought from somewhere lower, its true quality that of a distant despairing chorus, inverse sirens singing a warning from the deep. Marian edged around the brittle outcropping of black rock and peeked at the crevice; in sight a little further up and across from her position. Some of the rock above had been smashed away, as if something had impacted the tower and fallen downwards. Her best chance at discovering what had become of Meier was to get to the crevice and see if the submersible had indeed come to rest there.

She scaled the sharp rock, placing her hands carefully, her legs floating softly behind her. On closer inspection the crevice revealed itself to recess into the tower, the true extent of its depths hidden by the sharp black slivers of rock that encircled the entranceway.

To one side the splinters had been sheared away and a sizeable object sat: a sleek oval dome visible and outlined in shadow against the oscillating inky blues of the sea. She edged forwards, feeling her way towards the suspected submersible and a sudden movement erupted from the crevice. In one rush a huge shadow lifted from the black and bolted upwards. Part gliding and part scuttling, it left the domed object behind and raced around in the water, keeping to the general vicinity of the crevice behind it. Marian drew herself inwards, hoping to meld her frame to the rock in order to evade the creature's gaze. Aware that her presence had disturbed it she watched as it slowed and gracefully swam through the water, its omnidirectional eyestalks rotating urgently. The stomatopod, a species of giant mantis shrimp, sunk lower, its spindly forelegs clawing agitatedly as it propelled itself. She'd never observed one of such unusually massive proportions, and its shadow crept over her as big as a car. The intense flash of light, and following disruption to the water around her, upon her arrival suddenly made sense. She gazed up, frozen to her spot against the tower and noticed the similarity between the outline of the profile view of the stomatopod's carapace and the dome that sat motionless in the crevice. The colossal shrimp whipped one way then another, probing the water, its battle-scarred abdomen covered in fresh wounds secreting streamers of fleshy discharge.

Her arrival must have evoked a defensive response that caused the flash of light. A stomatopod's massive claws were designed to smash their combatants with a sharp impact, the snap so intense that it causes cavitation bubbles to form, as part of the inner mechanism, and collapse in a light-emitting pulse; this movement creates such force that a life-ending shockwave occurs in its aftermath. She'd been lucky, and the disruption that had sent her tumbling earlier had been nothing but a waning sideways glance. If she'd been hit head on, she'd be dead.

The light cable waved about invitingly. She was tempted to abandon Meier to his watery grave, especially as the creature had obviously pair-bonded itself to the submersible. It would not relinquish its prize easily; its propensity towards monogamy meaning that it would defend its mistaken mate with all it had at its disposal. One false move and she'd be impaled on one of its spear-like appendages, crushed by its gigantic clubbing claws, or ruptured by the full force of the resulting shockwave. Her career hopes becoming more remote—and all she'd worked for under threat when she resurfaced—she decided to proceed with her task. The cable was fitted with field recognition capabilities and would only need to be manoeuvred into place to bond to the submersible, extract it, and retract in order to ascend back to the research vessel. Katagi would take the acclaim and she'd quietly retain her position.

She edged back, determined to straddle the rear of the black tower and approach the crevice from the opposite side. The sharp slivers of rock were perfect to navigate, each making a readymade grappling handle. In no time she'd traversed the shady rear face and had her eyes on the crevice. From her new position the strained light beams filtering from above scattered across the contents of the small cave. The viewing window at the front of the submersible reflected the dull light sitting like mercury against the surrounding dark.

The stomatopod made bubble wakes as it searched the heights of the tower above her. Seizing her chance she propelled herself to the submersible.

She reached it by impacting the viewing window harshly and held herself in place by awkwardly attaching herself flatly to the glass with assistance from the attractive functioning of her suit. Meier sat before her inside. His body was still; his face flopped to one side, skin pale and purpled, with blood extruded from his ears, nose, eyes and mouth in dried trails. She guessed that he'd been hit by the stomatopod's shockwave, head on, before the submersible had settled on the dark tower and the creature had inexplicably chosen the defunct vessel as its partner.

A flash of light blinded her and she reeled backwards, away from the tower of rock. She scrambled forwards into the unknown, readying her body to withstand a harsh impact, but no shockwave followed in her direction. Another tower loomed out of the darkness ahead and she kicked her way frantically for it.

This column was less stable and littered with interconnected tunnels and openings. She grabbed at the side of it and landed on a section where the wall had been undermined by a colony of erosive deep-sea barnacles. Handfuls of solidified lava dislodged as she shifted her weight onto it. She glanced around to see that the stomatopod had responded to the disruption and was turning its segmented abdomen and flexing its swimmerets to guide itself towards her.

Without thought she dived into the depths of the unstable tower, a wide tunnel excavated into its innards by barnacle infestation. She turned on the illumination of her suit and the cavern lit up. Barnacles encased the sides in their thousands and created a throughway lined with pale white shells. She ploughed onwards, propelling through the murky organic detritus suspended in the trapped water of the tunnel. Loud cracking came from behind her and she turned to view the stomatopod forcing its way in, its gigantic claws breaking away the weakened rock and clustered barnacles of the entrance to the tunnel. Ahead, the tunnel narrowed and her exit appeared: a hole to the sea that she instantly observed was too small for her to fit through. She reached it and began hacking away at the barnacles covering its insides. The creature thrashed at the rock behind her and waves of disrupted water hit her as the shrimp intensified its efforts. It thrust its searching antenna forward and she spasmed out of its way as it poked at her back.

She bashed the surface layer of barnacles away and thrust her head into the hole. With a desperate wriggle she emerged from it into open water and headed for the glowing cable. Gracefully wavering and oblivious to her panic, the cable moved to meet her, attracted by her suit. In an instant she changed direction and led the tether straight to the quiet submersible, hurriedly guiding it to the sunken vessel. The cable initiated its bonding function, and the glow of its field insulation spread to encase the whole of the submersible. Marian moved upwards to hover above the vessel. Clinging to the cable, she began her own process of fixing her suit to the tether for the journey upwards.

She gazed down, eyes on the broken tower as streams of bubbles and clouds of dirt ejected from the hole she'd escaped from. A sharp lightning flash dazzled her. The upsweeping wails from the deep were interrupted by an almighty crack as the tower wobbled in response to the stomatopod's exploding shockwave. Its strength wasn't enough to topple the tower, and the creature didn't appear. Maybe the beast had trapped itself in the tunnel, or the reverberating shockwave had stopped it. Perhaps it was digging its way out and would emerge from the black any moment.

Attached to the cable, the first effects of her enforced half-sleep to the surface took hold. As her eyelids lowered involuntarily, she wondered if she'd make it all the way up—with Meier, with the submersible, with her career, and with her life. In panic, and accompanied by the symphonic movements of the deep, she closed her eyes.

ANIMAL UPRISING!

TAXIDERMY NIGHTMARE
Jacob Floyd

Jules stepped gently on the packed snow, trying to make as little sound as possible. He had been tracking some large deer prints for about twenty minutes and had yet to see the animal that left them, which was odd because he normally would have spotted his target by now. An accomplished hunter, he knew his way around the wild. No animal leaving such glaring tracks could elude him for long. Usually, they were as good as stuffed within ten minutes, twenty was a definite record.

"My hat's off to ya, pal," he said quietly, watching the puff of his breath swirl in the air.

Jules didn't wait in tree stands or shooting houses for the kill to cross his path. He was an old-school tracker who preferred to face the animal on the ground. That's how he'd always hunted, and he had taken many trophies that way.

He started with the simple creatures: beavers, squirrels, rabbits, birds. Once he'd lost interest in easy prey, he progressed to deer, owls, and hawks. Soon, those too offered little challenge. He then spent three years in Alaska hunting grey wolves. His last kill there was his favorite: a nearly twelve-hundred pound Kodiak bear.

Jules considered the day he brought down that bear to be the greatest of his hunting career. He vividly remembered every detail: the hours spent cautiously tracking the giant killer, with an exhilarating fear flowing through his body; how its back was turned the moment he came upon it. He whistled to get its attention, refusing to shoot the beast from behind; he wanted to make eye contact and let the animal know who the superior predator was. When the Kodiak saw him, it roared and stood up. Jules then raised his Ruger Hawkeye Alaskan and fired into the bear. He'd aimed for the shoulder but hit the upper-left portion of its torso.

That had only angered the beast and made it charge. Jules had to run to take up another position. When he fired again, the Ruger shell went right into the Kodiak's shoulder, shattering it and hitting the vitals before splattering through the other side. The bear kept coming even though it was clearly losing life. Jules, always the roughneck, pulled his seven-foot iron bear spear and charged the creature. The two converged on one another and Jules, with all the strength his massive frame could muster, drove the weapon right into the bear's chest, dealing out the death blow. But Jules did not escape unscathed. During the collision, the bear struck out, landing a glancing blow across Jules's torso, ripping mighty claw marks through his jacket, vest, and shirt, and tearing some skin from his chest. The blow caused Jules to release the spear and it sent him rolling. The Kodiak sailed forward, landing on the spear and dying.

When Jules recovered his wits, he walked to the bear and looked at him with a smile.

"You are an awesome creature," he said. "But nothing like Jules Hancock."

The glory of such a kill!

His friends did not believe his account. They were so accustomed to telling tall tales of their own that they immediately assumed Jules had done the same. Although the spear wound was clear to see, as was the scar across his chest, they insisted that he had speared the bear after shooting it dead and now he was just putting them on. Jules, a man unperturbed by the opinions of lesser warriors, just smiled and said, "Have it your way." And that always left them wondering.

To have defeated such a creature left Jules feeling indestructible. From that point on, hunting wild game was his life. He had gained local notoriety for it and hoped to become known on a global level. His next expedition would be to East Africa where he could hunt the greatest of animals, the powerful and monstrously beautiful: lions, rhinos, elephants, tigers, and any other beast that crossed his path. He wanted them all for his cabin; he could imagine the mighty heads jutting out from his wall.

But those days lay ahead of him. For now, he would content himself with this rather large deer he was following. Earlier that day, he had scouted the remote area in the wooded hills of eastern Kentucky near his cabin and saw the standard signs of your average deer, but nothing quite like this. Judging by the size of the splayed tracks he'd found, he was tailing an unusually large buck. The tracks looked to be six or seven inches long and possibly between five and six inches wide. The path the creature walked was peculiar, as it displayed no sign of zigzags or leaps.

Jules pictured this animal as a tall, powerful buck majestically walking through the snow, like a king of the forest, head held high, black eyes watching the landscape with regal indifference with no idea that the greatest hunter among men was tracking him. He envisioned coming upon it, standing at a curve in one of the hills, looking at the land below, its great and mighty antlers cutting an impressive silhouette against the icy morning sky. Of course, Jules would not shoot it in the back. This deer deserved too much respect for that. Jules would issue his customary warning whistle and when the courageous creature turned, he would put a bullet right in its belly and finish it off with his machete.

When Jules hunted, his mentality was that of the wild beasts he sought: cruel, savage, barbaric. Simply pulling the trigger and walking away was not his style. It was too easy. He wanted to get his hands dirty with the blood of the battle. To do it any other way was a cheap victory.

Minutes passed and the winter wind blew icy flakes of snow off the naked branches around him. The sound of it disrupted his hearing, which had been attentively tuned to the wilderness, waiting on any indication that the deer was near. He stopped to wait for the rustling trees to be still.

When the woods were once again silent, Jules moved on, following the hoof prints into a shaded path where the brush grew thick and clogged the passage. He stopped to peer into the dimly lit area, looking at the ground to see if the prints had stopped. They had not. They continued pushing beyond his line of sight.

Jules stepped to the edge of the small trees and large bushes to examine the undergrowth. Nothing had been disturbed. No branches or bushes, high or low, were broken. If the deer had passed through here, which the prints indicated it had, then it had done so without causing any damage to the fragile nature in its path.

Remarkable, Jules thought. *That is damn near impossible for such a large creature. What grace it must possess!*

This new development only enriched the pursuit and made him more determined to topple the beast. He ducked his right shoulder and pushed at the brush with his right hand, turning his 85 Sako Finnlight long-ways towards his chest, pressing it to his body as he pushed his way through. Though he kept his eyes on the woods, he couldn't help but steal a glance at his weapon, admiring the beauty of the black, fluted barrel. Such a narrow and lightweight thing, yet it packed a death-punch capable of bringing down almost any animal.

He had many rifles for many hunts and he kept them in perfect condition, mounted and labeled in his gun room. They were equally beautiful as the heads on his walls and the bodies in his cabin—most of the bodies, anyway.

In the last two years, he had taken up hybrid taxidermy art, using mostly the smaller animals. He had placed turtle shells on squirrel bodies and stitched goose necks to them. He had sewn bird wings onto chipmunks and even given some of them cat legs. Yes, he had hunted strays, too: dogs and cats, mostly. He placed a Rottweiler head on a doe, and a cat's arms on a possum. He even sewed a rooster head onto a rabbit and gave it swan wings. Such strange creations fascinated him, and the fact that he had the power to make them gave even deeper purpose to his hunts. He ended the mundane lives of these animals and transformed them into something unnaturally beautiful. To them, he was like God.

Yes, what a notion that he could be like God. "Hear that my boy?" he whispered to the elusive buck. "God is coming."

He walked through the brush and into a clearing beneath a thin roof of empty branches. Beyond that, several yards away, that pale winter sky shone through the trees. It grew warmer where Jules stood, and the deer prints dissipated in the slush of a large path melted through the snow. There was a strange aroma, almost like spring, in the air, too. The smell of fresh pine and clean water overpowered the harsh scent of winter.

Checking along the ground, he saw the path of the hooves indented into the soft earth. Jules leveled his Sako, ready to shoot, and followed the track to the edge of the clearing. He stepped beyond the tangled branches and found himself standing on a cliff overlooking a valley of snow-dusted trees. The spring-time aromas grew stronger and the cold air rushed his lungs as he breathed them in. He looked down once more, picturing himself as God again, looking at the world below.

"King of the mountain," he said.

ANIMAL UPRISING!

A soft noise like a whisper to his right caught his attention. He looked, and gasped when he saw the source. Standing at the edge of the cliff, looking out over the valley, just as Jules had previously pictured, was the creature he'd been trailing. Only the deer was not as he imagined. It was much more; it was beyond comprehension.

The magnificent creature stood every bit of nine feet tall, and had to weigh over a thousand pounds. Its noble countenance turned to face Jules, temporarily freezing him in awe. The diminutive tail did not move and the long ears rose as if to hear Jules's thoughts. The antlers extended from its head, several feet, like wide, powerful arms with three-clawed hands at their ends reaching towards the Heavens. But, despite how impressive its physical stature was, that was not what seized Jules. The creature, from head to toe, was pure silver, and it shimmered, even in the weak glow of the winter sun.

Jules blinked several times, thinking the sparkling creature would return to normal each time he opened his eyes. But it continued to shine, like a river glimmering in summertime. This creature was one-of-a-kind; it was royalty; it was undoubtedly divine.

"And it will be an even greater prize than the Kodiak," he said and took aim.

The deer did not attempt to run; it did not attempt to fight. It simply looked at Jules and waited. When the bullet pierced its chest, a burst of silver light erupted at the edge of the cliff.

Jules was temporarily blinded and he threw his hands in front of his eyes, dropping the Finnlight. He stumbled back, tripped on a tree root, and fell. The gunshot echoed through the hills, bouncing from one side of the valley to the other. The impact of the silver explosion rattled the trees and the ground. Jules felt the vibrations running beneath him. He lay for several seconds trying to regain his vision. Once it returned to him, he thought he saw hundreds of sparkling lights floating to the ground like confetti. Sitting up, he closed his eyes and shook off the blow.

When he stood again, he saw the silver deer lying motionless near the cliff's edge. His Finnlight lay a few feet to his right, so he retrieved it and walked over to his prey, ready to fire again if necessary.

The carcass lay on its left side, not breathing, and its eyes were open and lifeless. But there was no blood; only scatterings of the silver

62

substance stained the land around it. Jules knelt to be sure the deer was dead. No pulse, the kill was complete. He touched some of the silver liquid with his gloved hands and brought it to his nose—pine and water, just like the smell that had been in the air.

"How strange," he mused and wiped the substance on the ground. Standing up, he said, "Time to get you home."

Gonna be a hell of a haul, he thought.

Jules had a large black utility sled that could haul just about anything, but the buck was huge and would be a tight fit. He considered cutting off its legs but dismissed that idea quickly. This stag was too singular to desecrate. No one had seen a truly silver deer before, not like this, he was certain of that. This was going on display in full form right beside the Kodiak. It was going home whole, with its legs bound and tucked inside the sled. He could work out the stiffness later. Hauling that heavy beast was going to make for an arduous trek down the hill, but Jules was a powerful man, and he was going to get his workout today.

By the time Jules retrieved the sled and rope from the wagon hitched to the back of his truck and dragged the deer back down the hill, it was almost nightfall. The sky had grown a deep blue while he secured the catch in the wagon. As he pulled off towards home, he was watching Orion emerge in the winter sky.

Once home, he pulled the deer into the work room located at the back of his spacious, eleven-room cabin. The room consisted of a pegboard covered in tools, various taxidermy animals, a concrete floor, and several work tables and tubs to hold discarded innards and body parts. He admired the splendid creature before turning off the light and closing the door. He looked forward to working on it, but it would have to wait. He was sore and exhausted. The pain he didn't mind; he could work through that. But a tired mind meant sloppy work and he would not risk messing up that magnificent deer.

He hit the shower, turning the water up as hot as it would go, making his thick skin turn pink. The entire room was as steamy as a sauna by the time he had toweled off and gotten dressed for bed. The hot mist rolled from the room and into the hallway when he opened the door and went to the kitchen to make hot tea. Coffee was no good right now because he needed to rest. He couldn't have fitful sleep before the important project that awaited him.

As he drank the tea he strolled to his taxidermy room and admired the trophies and abominations he'd made. The three-legged cat with a possum tail peered at him menacingly. Next to it, a parakeet head on a chipmunk body that had rabbit feet stared out blankly. He admired his art for awhile before leaving the room and heading to bed.

Jules lay for awhile excited about his new addition. He couldn't wait to get to work on it, and all he could think about was how majestic it would look alongside his other prizes. Many minutes passed before he was able to calm his thoughts and drift into sleep.

He dreamed himself back on the hill, stepping through the snow once again. The pine-and-water scent filled the air, pulling him along the path. His Sako was in his hand and he could see the giant deer tracks on the ground before him. He followed them and soon found himself emerging once again from the shaded tangle onto the chilly hillside. The silver deer stood at the edge, as before, shining over the valley.

This time Jules hesitated. An awesome presence weighed upon him as the cloud of silver sparkles drifted his way. He wanted to raise the gun, but found himself arrested by a mixture of fear and serenity. His arms shook and the rifle trembled in his hands. The cloud came upon him and immense fright screamed for him to flee—but he couldn't. He watched in horror as the twinkling sphere engulfed him, washing his body in a cold liquid that was like air softly blowing against his skin. The feeling calmed his spirit and killed the fear. He became lightheaded and felt as if he was fading, but not from life, from the pain and weakness of mortality. Once he was entirely immersed within the mass, the stag turned to face him.

Destroyer, it said in a deep, strong voice. *You may murder the flesh, but your power stops there. Your threat ends now. Leave from here and take your twisted heart, for I am now the keeper of your spirit.*

The silver cloud began to pull away, tugging at Jules's skin. As it floated from him, his flesh tore slowly. Cracks spread across his epidermis, then into his dermis. Jules screamed as the skin was ripped from his body. The sky grew a dark blue, making the deer shine brighter.

Your transgressions are abundant, and now it is I you must answer to. I shall judge your sins.

Jules's body was torn down the middle before he woke up in the cold darkness of his bedroom. No light, save for that from the clock at his bedside, could be seen. When he closed his eyes he could still see faint sparks of silver. It took a few seconds for them to fade, and when they did, Jules sat up in bed. Leaning on his hands, he listened to the stillness. For a second, he thought he could smell a hint of water and pine. He shivered thinking of the silver stag's words in his dream.

After the nightmare wore off, he fell back on his bed and pulled his thin sheet up to his neck. He had almost fallen back to sleep a few minutes later when he felt something poke gently against his left calf. He opened his eyes but didn't move, thinking that he had imagined it. A few seconds later, he felt something crawling along his right shin and up to the knee.

Jules kicked his leg violently, knocking whatever had been crawling on him to the floor. It thumped on the wood and made a continuous scraping sound as it started moving slowly through the darkened room. Sitting up in bed again, he turned his ear towards the sound to be sure of what he was hearing. Undoubtedly, there was something small scratching along his floor.

He quickly leaned toward the bedside table, picked up his phone, and shined its light in the direction of the sound. At first he could not make out what he was seeing. It was something dark dragging itself slowly across the floor. It was less than a foot long and without any girth. Deciding it was nothing to be afraid of, he threw back the sheet and got out of bed to inspect it.

That strange smell of pine and water suddenly wafted through the room, causing him to stop and turn towards the bedroom door, which was cracked open. A strange light in the living room beyond was finding its way through the narrow slit. Jules squinted to see it clearer. The light looked to be silver and it was sweeping around the living room like a light tower spotlight.

"Who's out there?" he said, walking towards the door.

Before he made it across the bedroom, something squeaked on the floor behind him. He stopped and noticed the scratching sound had ceased. Forgetting the silver light, he went back to the thing on the floor. When he shined the light upon it again, he felt a chill pass through him. Looking up at him, with what should have been dead black eyes, was the head of a small rabbit attached to the body of a squirrel. The abomination had rolled onto its back and was kicking its two hind legs. The front legs had been replaced by bat wings, and they were twitching slightly against the floor.

"What the hell?" Jules said, bringing the phone closer to illuminate the creature better.

What lay there on the floor before him was identical to one of his taxidermy pets. But, they were dead. There was no way that's what this was.

When he brought the light closer to the hybrid he saw that he was wrong. Tiny stitches were sewn into the body where the foreign parts had been added, and it was undeniably his work. But how could this be? He had removed all the innards from each animal. There's no way one could survive. But the body was moving, the mouth was squeaking, and the black eyes had life in them.

"No way this is happening," he said and reached down to pick the animal up.

When his fingers touched the creature's body, it screeched and bit him hard, catching his index and middle fingers in its mouth. He grunted in pain and pulled back his hand, but the little animal remained attached, biting down harder. Jules screamed and shook his hand, dropping his phone and slinging the animal away. It took some of the finger flesh with it and Jules's digits were soon dripping blood all over the floor.

He quickly went into the bathroom next to his bedroom and cleaned his tiny wounds. There was a box of gauze in the cabinet attached to the wall and he pulled it out to wrap his fingers. When done, he went back into the bedroom to find the little monster and finish it off. When he flicked on the light, it was nowhere to be seen.

"Where you at, you little shit?"

A loud bang from beyond the bedroom door stole his attention. The silver light was now glaring, and the aroma of spring had returned stronger than before. He took the new edition Model 1873 Winchester rifle from the wall next to his bed, went to the door, prepared to investigate the sound, but stopped just as his hand grabbed the doorknob.

Turning around about halfway, he visually searched the room again. Still, there was no sign of the reanimated animal.

Where had it gone?

Jules soon concluded that it was not one of his taxidermy creatures. He had imagined that because his mind wasn't right after coming out of a deep sleep. What he had actually encountered was a normal woodland creature that had gotten into his house and bit him when he tried to remove it. It had been a long day in the hills, and he had suffered a heavy blow after shooting that peculiar stag. He had simply been rattled a bit. Now, he had to find out what was going on in his cabin, so he opened the bedroom door and stepped from the room.

Ahead of him, the silver light shined from the kitchen beyond the living room, no longer sweeping the area but only pulsing lightly. It lit a bright path across the room and the springtime scent seemed to be growing stronger. A rustling sound came from the darkened hallway behind him and he turned to see if anyone was there. Only the empty darkness greeted him.

He looked around to see if he could find what had caused the loud thump. As he drew nearer to the kitchen, he looked towards the wall to his right and saw that one of the large deer heads he had mounted long ago was missing.

He then chuckled and thought, *That's what that noise was, just the head falling off the wall. It has been up so long it must have come loose.*

A large white wraparound couch surrounded the area where the head had fallen, and the chaise lounge on the left side of it blocked his way. He stepped around it and crossed the floor. The silver light hit the ceiling suddenly and Jules stopped to watch it slide across the room before disappearing. He now stood in the dark with whatever bizarre occurrences were taking place. Instinctively, he started to move across the room to turn on the light, but stopped when he heard a strange wheezing coming from behind the couch.

The sound lasted only a few seconds and he shivered slightly until it stopped. Jules then began to relax in the silence. But when the wheezing was replaced by a weak bleating noise, he went cold all over because it was a sound he knew so well. It was the bleating of a deer, and the wheezing had been a warning to other deer that something was wrong.

The wheezing began again and Jules stepped behind the couch to see what was causing it. Behind there, he saw a dark shape on the floor. Letting his rifle dangle at his side, he knelt down to get a closer look at what lay before him. A small amount of moonlight filtering in through the windows and glass double-doors a few feet away made it easier for Jules to see what was making the sounds. When Jules leaned over and saw what it was, he gasped and fell back. On the floor in front of him, the fallen deer head had come to life, its mouth moving as it continued to bleat.

"What?" was all Jules could say.

The head began to flop around. The deer's black eyes stared at Jules as the mouth opened wide and began to hack and cough. Jules, stunned beyond words or thought, raised his rifle, ready to fire at the resurrected head.

Before he could pull the trigger, the living room was bathed in that powerful silver glow. Jules dropped the Winchester and spun around on his butt to see the source. At first, he had to hold his hand in front of his face to shield his eyes. In seconds, the light had faded into a soft shine with little stars twinkling in the air, reflecting off the walls like the shimmers of a disco ball.

Jules turned his head towards the kitchen where the light emanated from. His eyes widened in shock at the sight before him. There at threshold of the room stood the silver stag with the glow of its aura pulsating around it. Its angry and accusing black eyes glared at Jules in judgment and Jules felt the sting of its wrath.

"What the hell?"

I am the Protector of the Forest, the stag spoke to Jules telepathically. *You are a threat to all the creatures that live within it.*

"But I shot you," he said, going for his rifle again.

I cannot be killed. I was sent to see that you pay for your transgressions against the sacred spirits of the woods.

Jules picked up his rifle and jumped to his feet.

"Bullshit," he said, then aimed and squeezed the trigger.

The shell exploded through the air, racing towards the deer. When it hit the glowing creature, another bright explosion happened. Jules braced himself for the aftershock, but this time it did not come. The light expanded like a force field and shattered the slug on impact, sending blinding ripples of shining silver across the room. The rifle began to burn in Jules's hands so he dropped it.

Never more than once will your attacks work against me, the deer said. *And never more than once will your attacks work against those you have already slain.*

A loud bang came from one of the rooms down the hallway diagonal from where Jules stood. It was followed by the sound of something breaking against the floor. Scratches and bumps reverberated through the room. Jules looked around and saw heads moving about on the walls and taxidermy animals stirring on the shelves.

Those who slept now wake, said the deer. *Your judgment is imminent.*

As the stag spoke, its mouth emitted a sparkling stream of silver that broke apart and floated towards Jules's trophies. Within minutes, each dead animal was wrapped in a shroud of shining light. Jules watched in horror as the creatures began to twitch and thrash about. He backed away, turning slowly as he went, to survey the full nightmare coming to life around him.

You cannot escape, said the stag, but Jules didn't hear.

One of the owls on a shelf to Jules's left shrieked and flew from its spot. Its physical wings remained still, but in their place appeared the transparent image of silver wings, flapping gracefully, carrying the owl towards Jules's face.

Jules managed to get his arm up just before the owl's claws could rip off a chunk of his face. It took a small hunk from his forearm, causing it to drip blood from a shallow wound. He screamed and fell against the wall to his right and watched as other winged animals took flight.

A falcon from which he had removed the eyes came at him, ghostly silver eyes in the darkened sockets now trained upon him. It landed on his shoulders and struck out at his head with its beak. Two raven-crow hybrids fashioned from the same two birds—both having been split in half to have each of their respective halves fused with that of the other—were carried across the room on a current of silver light. They began pecking and clawing at Jules. The worst of all was the hawk with the small goat horn attached to its head. It rushed Jules and speared him in the right side, driving the horn mercilessly through the flesh, stabbing at one of his ribs.

"Fuck!" Jules cried out.

He grabbed the hawk and tried to pull it away. Its ghostly wings flapped furiously, struggling against his grip. Jules wrestled through the agony and was able to yank the bird away, dislodging the unforgiving goat horn from his body. Once the horn was removed, the gaping hole spewed blood down his side. He threw down the hawk and grabbed the wound. The flow of blood was warm and sticky against his hand, and with each movement he thought he would collapse. If he did, however, he knew he would be ripped to shreds by his vengeful assailants.

The birds had begun an aviary assault that Jules could not stave off. Ignoring the howling pain in his side, he retreated towards the door at the back of the room as the angry creatures, revived and empowered by the spiritual light, unleashed their furious onslaught upon his flesh. After suffering several more puncture wounds and knocking the birds from his body, he made it to the door. He entered the room, closed the door, and leaned against the backside to catch his breath. He slid down to the floor, leaving blood streaks on the wood.

The birds started banging and clawing at the other side of the door, shrieking and trying to break through. Jules crawled quickly away and watched fixedly for a few seconds, fearful they might gain entry. They stopped after a few minutes as the silver light began to pour through the cracks of the door, bringing with it the familiar aroma.

Patches of glimmering silver began to materialize through the wood, and soon the stag was standing in front of the doorway, peering down at Jules.

You cannot escape your judgment.

The light bathed the room as it had the last, heading for the four-legged woodland creatures and abominations Jules had captured inside. The doe he had given the Rottweiler head was in here, as well as a fox, a wolf, and a bobcat. As they came to life, Jules came to the realization that a grisly death was in store for him if he did not move.

He stood up and rushed for the gun cabinet along the back wall. The deer might not be able to be killed, but he was damn sure going to see if the other animals could be. He slid open the glass and grabbed his Beretta 9000, already loaded, and held it out, ready for the creatures to attack.

The fox was the first to engage; swaddled in silver, it ran at him with its teeth bared. Jules fired two shots that drove the fox back but did not stop it. By the time the second shot was fired, the wolf and bobcat were coming. Jules fired at them too and got the same results. He emptied the magazine into the converging animals, sending silver sparks exploding through the room. They fell to the floor but did not die, and were back on their feet in seconds.

The Rott-doe hybrid was now stamping across the floor. Its movements were awkward because the head was too big for the neck, but the stag's silver magic carried it onward. Its menacing Rottweiler mouth showed Jules teeth fit to maim, and those fangs were meant for him.

Jules had no time to pull another gun from the cabinet, so he turned and bolted towards the backroom. Before he made it, the Rott's head tore into his backside, ripping flesh from his lower back, and causing him to slip and fall into the room. The doorway was narrow and the creature banged against the frame and fell down, blocking the other three from entering.

Jules rushed to the door and slammed it shut. He was now in the backmost room of the cabin, which was his den, so-to-speak. There was a small television, even though he didn't care much for TV, some bookshelves, and a table in the middle where he cleaned his guns. A long table with tools and magazines rested along the wall adjacent to the door, and he mustered all the strength his blood-oozing body could to pull that heavy piece of furniture in front of the door.

He knew the deer would squeeze its way through the door again, like the T-1000 from *Terminator 2,* and with the way the other creatures were pounding against it, it was only a matter of time before they busted through. He searched the room for a plan, and he saw what he needed.

Leaning against the wall on the other side of the room was his trump card: his Holland & Holland .700 Nitro Express double rifle; its box of slugs was sitting on the floor next to it. It was old school, but he loved it. The beastly elephant gun could bring down anything. He rarely used it, and he was saving it for his African safari. But today was a special circumstance, to say the least. Today was a desperate time. He snatched the cannon up, bent over, grabbed the ammo, and stood up. When he stood, he froze, for he found himself looking into the eyes of the monster in the glass case next to where the gun had lain.

Jules's eyes met the great Kodiak's. For many seconds he remained still, except for his hand, which trembled at the thought of the stag bringing that creature back to life. Hanging on the wall on the other side of the case was the iron spear he'd used to impale the behemoth. The glass of the case was several inches thick. If the deer barged into the room and brought the beast back to life, perhaps the bear could not free itself.

As if hearing his thoughts, the room began to take on a silver hue and a springtime scent once again filled the air as the spirit animal pushed its way through the door.

I see the thought has already come to you, said the deer. *Your greatest kill – yes?*

Jules swallowed and closed his eyes. Slowly, he turned his head in the direction of the unwanted visitor and opened them again.

"Yes, my greatest kill."

Yes. Indeed.

The deer blinked three times and large beams of silver shot from its eyes. The light found its way through the glass and seeped into the body of the Kodiak. Jules's stomach began to twist as small embers of life began to ignite in the creature's eyes.

Your time draws to an end, the deer said.

The bear's claws began to tap, and the mouth started to twitch. Immersed in the stag's glow, the body began to soften and move. It shook its head, moved its legs, and the glass case began to rattle.

On the other side of the door, the other beasts were pounding away, shaking the frame, causing cracks to form in it. That door was strong, but not strong enough to hold them all back. He turned and watched the door shake and began to load his rifle.

The deer stared at him with emotionless eyes. *This is the hour of your judgment. You will not escape it.*

"Maybe not," he said. "But I won't go without a fight."

As he was putting the slugs into the gun, a brain-shattering roar from behind him caused him to jump and drop a bullet. He stepped away and turned, seeing that the Kodiak had returned to life. When the roar ceased, the animals on the other side of the door abandoned their plight.

The bear lowered its head and stared at Jules. When their eyes met, Jules felt rage and hatred radiating from the creature, and it seeped into his soul.

He remembers you, said the stag. *Animals dream in death, just like the souls of man, awaiting their next journey. In that lingering darkness, he has thought of nothing but the man that brought him into it. He has longed for nothing more than his revenge. Now, he shall have it.*

The bear roared again and raised its paw and began battering the glass. The case rocked and small cracks formed in the corners. It then took to head-butting its cell, causing longer, deeper cracks. With shaking hands, Jules went back to loading his rifle.

Fate will now judge you. You must face your sins. Do not run. We will be waiting for you on the other side.

As the deer vanished back through the door, it sent one last stream of silver towards the case. The bear had been rocking its body against the interior, causing spider web cracks all over it. As the silver light approached the case, the bear stopped and watched it eagerly. Jules watched in terror. Setting the ammo down on the floor, he rushed past the case and grabbed the spear from the wall. He would only be able to get off one or two shots before that monster was upon him, and he had a sneaking suspicion it would not die.

It felt like slow-motion hell watching that damn deer's ray of silver sail towards the case. Jules positioned himself by the door, ready to blow the bear away as soon as it came busting through the glass. When the silver touched the case, like a long pale finger extended from the hand of Death, it shattered in a salvo of glass and silver showers. The bear wasted no time. Roaring like the winds of Hell, its nightmarish silver form trundled towards Jules.

One shot eliminated all sound in the room as the shells slammed into the cranium right between the eyes of the Kodiak, throwing silver light everywhere. The beast fell back and its mouth opened and its head vibrated, but Jules could not hear it due to the pounding deafness in his ears.

Jules, too, had been sent backwards. He was the right size to fire such a mighty weapon, but the kick still pushed him against the wall. In the fury of the moment, he hadn't braced himself well enough before firing and he found himself bouncing off the wall and hitting the floor. He managed to hang onto the rifle. The ammo lay next to him, so he took out two more slugs and jammed them into the gun.

The bear shook its head and Jules fired again, this time right in the chest. More silver sparks burst forth as the bear fell hard onto its back. The kick from the rifle felt like it damn near tore his arm off. He put two more slugs in and struggled to his feet. With his arm in severe pain, he widened his stance and aimed carefully. The bear sat up and rolled to get back on its feet. Jules aimed for its chest again and fired, slamming two slugs into its face. Surely this would be enough to drop the gargantuan.

But it was not. Instead of shattering the animal's skull as they should have, the shells hit a barrier of silver light that rippled like a pond beneath a fallen leaf, causing no damage to the target. The bear was angry and its eyes gave away its next move: to rip Jules to shreds.

Jules's arm was numb and his head felt blitzed. There was no way he could manage to fire that monstrous Holland & Holland again. The spear was on the floor next to him, so he knelt to pick it up. It felt heavier than it should have, no doubt as a result of the titanic blasts from his rifle. But, he sucked in a breath and swallowed the pain. The room was not that big and the bear was now coming. He knelt and leveled the spear. When the bear roared again, Jules was glad to be nearly deaf from the gunshots, because it did not shake him.

As the bear drew in, Jules pushed himself upwards, driving the spear towards the bear's throat as hard as he could. His aim was true. The silver shield did not deflect the thrust. When the bear came down at him, the tip pressed into the flesh with an unsettling crunch, like jamming a knife into papier-mâché. There was no blood, but silver light oozed from the wound. The bear reared back and the spear went with him. Jules tightened his grip as hard as he could, trying to wrench the weapon free. The bear thrashed about with the spear in his throat, yanking Jules left and right. After a few seconds of struggle, the bear turned to the side with such power that Jules was flung across the room, tap-dancing the whole way, until he was sent sprawling along the floor.

The spear was still stuck in the bear's throat. The creature noticed it and grabbed the shaft between his paws. Slowly, he pulled the weapon out and let it fall. The clang of the heavy metal on the wooden floor was Jules's death knell.

The bear dropped to all fours, eyeing Jules as he made his slow march across the floor. Jules, the mighty hunter, pissed his pants as he watched the Leviathan's torturous approach. Tiny specks of silver sparkled in the bear's stiff fur. His eyes were black and vacant, except for the tiny glimmer of vengeful malice twinkling within.

The bear was just feet in front of Jules now, its imposing shadow looming over him. Jules, slobbering, crying, and shivering, balled up his fists, prepared to land at least one blow before in his inevitable evisceration.

"Come on, you son of a bitch," he stammered weakly.

Just when he was beginning to feel brave, the giant Kodiak rose up on its hind paws, lifted its arms, and bellowed a roar of death that shook the room. Jules could hear it, ever so faintly; enough to make both his fists and his balls shrivel into nothing.

When the roar ended, the bear looked down at Jules. It took a couple steps forward and began to descend. When it came down, its front claws slid right into Jules's body like it was nothing more than a balloon. Jules screamed and the bear opened its mouth and closed its jaws on his head. His arms twitched and his legs thrashed as the bear took its revenge.

The slaughter did not take long. In the room just beyond, the stag and the rest of Jules's victims stood still, awaiting the deed to be done. A few minutes later, the bear knocked down the door and stood before them, blood smeared in his fur and dripping from his mouth.

The bear and the stag stared at each other. Retribution had been rendered. The animals would no longer be trapped by spiritual unrest. Their bodies would have to return to their tombs inside, but their souls were free to go.

You may go now, it said to the Kodiak, and the bear turned and headed back into the cabin.

The silver stag led the others back inside and watched as they each returned to their resting places. After their bodies had gone back to sleep, the cabin filled with numerous silver lights that soon floated into the wilderness. The deer followed those lights outside and stood in the snow, guiding the souls, speaking to each one, leading them through the door to the other side.

Coyotes descended from the hills, smelling the blood of man. They came from the shadows of the trees and stopped when they saw the glowing deer before them. Their first instinct was to attack, and they growled. The deer turned to face them, saying nothing. The coyote pack soon recoiled and went into the cabin to find their feast.

The stag willed a little more hunger and power to the coyotes. Jules would soon be reduced to nothing but broken bones. It then turned back to watch the souls ascend, and felt content once the last of them vanished into the sky.

A few seconds later, the smell of pine and water wafted through the winter air as the snow suddenly whisked around the creature. The stag began to break down into small shards of shining silver that melded with the whirling snowdrift. Before the mysterious wind died down, a little silver whirlwind spun into the air and disappeared with one last bright pop.

THE FOX
Judith Baron

The rain started pouring on his minivan. Fifty-seven-year-old construction worker Jacky Wu turned on the radio. The eight o'clock news came on and the newscaster reported that a Category 1 typhoon was approaching Hong Kong. Jacky started heading south from Causeway Bay toward Aberdeen to call it a night after a thirteen-hour work day, passing the Happy Valley Racecourse when he spotted what looked like a limping four-legged animal on the sidewalk. For a split second he thought it was glowing red; maybe it was the glare from the traffic lights and headlights, or maybe he was just plain tired. Two dogs trailed the animal about ten feet behind, whimpering and barking at it repeatedly, sounding as if they weren't sure whether the injured creature was friend or foe.

When Jacky's headlights shone on the limping animal, he was shocked to discover that it was not a dog but a fox. It was red, slightly smaller than the two dogs, and though he wasn't an expert in animals, Jacky did not think foxes existed in the wild of Hong Kong. Did it escape from the zoo? Or was it abandoned by a scofflaw who smuggled and kept wildlife as pets? There was a marbled fox that someone brought to the zoo a few months ago, where it stayed until they found it a home in Singapore. Maybe this was a case similar to that.

The fox slowed down and stopped moving forward. Then suddenly, it just dropped to the ground. The dogs continued to bark and pace back and forth around it.

Jacky had seen some documentaries in which people saved injured animals by bringing them to an animal hospital. He supposed he should call the police and leave it to them, but in this weather, an injured animal probably wasn't a priority for the cops. There was also the pressing matter

77

of the stray dogs. He was raised a Buddhist and had compassion for all living things. He pulled over to the side of the road and took out a blanket from the backseat. He shooed the two dogs away. They were acting strange; it was almost as if they wanted to draw attention to the fox.

"Okay, okay! I see it!" Jacky said to the dogs.

Maybe they wanted the spoils of war. Thankfully, they scampered off without a fight. Jacky was getting wet, and managed to wrap the blanket over the listless fox and then carry it back to his minivan.

He put the fox in the backseat. It was still breathing, but just barely. It looked at Jacky and didn't struggle, which was a relief. He didn't want to be attacked by an injured wild animal and get rabies.

Jacky sneezed as he got soaked by the rain, and also because the fox had a very strong musky odour that got more pungent the wetter it got. The fox whimpered a bit, so at least it was still alive, but Jacky would have to find help for it fast. He reached into the cup holder near the gear shift for loose change to pay the toll for the Aberdeen Tunnel. There was a zoo on the way to where he was going and he could call for help there. Hopefully there would be emergency veterinary staff still onsite. He would have better luck with a private corporation than a government department.

Jacky pulled up to the toll plaza. He gave the exact change and entered the tunnel. The wind was picking up outside and the street lights in the tunnel began flickering. Just as he hoped to himself that the power wouldn't go out, everything suddenly went black. It then became eerily dark, despite the headlights from the other cars in the tunnel.

"Aiya! I hate it when that happens!" Jacky muttered aloud in Cantonese and glanced in the rear-view mirror at the fox. He had to do a double take because for a moment, he thought he saw the fox glowing red again, but this time with quite a few tails sticking up.

What the hell was that?

Jacky's heart skipped a beat, and the lights couldn't have come back on at a better moment. When he looked in the rear-view mirror again, the fox was still wrapped in its blanket with no extra tails sticking out the back.

Jacky rubbed his eyes and looked again. He must have been so tired that his eyes were playing tricks on him. At that point, he was more concerned about whether the fox would survive before it got to the zoo, or if he could find help at all at this hour and in this weather.

The lights flickered yet again, and within seconds, the power in the tunnel went out a second time. This time he clearly saw a glowing red fox in the backseat, with not one but several tails sticking out of the blanket.

Jacky screamed. He tried to remember all the folklore he knew as a child about fox spirits—they were demons and could shapeshift, and usually did so in the guise of beautiful women.

Why did this one not appear as a beautiful woman? he wondered.

At a time like this how could he possibly get sidetracked by these thoughts? Well, he hadn't had a girlfriend in years...and at his age, he had pretty much given up hope.

Focus, Jacky!

He snapped out of his digression so he could think and act quickly.

He replayed all the Asian soap operas and movies he'd seen about fox spirits in his head. What were the motives of the spirits? He remembered that they could use dark magic and deceive you. They would devour humans whole or eat their hearts to gain their knowledge and wisdom. The ultimate goal of a fox spirit was to become an immortal, celestial fox because nothing could destroy it.

The requirements of attaining immortality varied. In South Korean folklore, the more wisdom the fox spirit learned, the more tails it gained; but the limit was capped at nine, hence the moniker "nine-tailed fox". In Chinese folklore, a thousand-year-old fox spirit would gain all of its nine tails and achieve immortality, so it seemed to be earned by just surviving to a ripe old age (of a thousand years).

Jacky looked at the fox behind him and counted the tails he could see: one, two, three, four, five, six, seven...and eight! If the fox spirit were to eat him now, would it gain its ninth tail and become immortal? Wait, he's not that smart...he was a terrible student and barely finished high school. He might just count as half a human when it came to wisdom and knowledge.

He took the exit to the zoo. Upon the exit with street lights, the fox was in its original form. Jacky wondered if he imagined the red glow and the eight tails. He was exhausted. He had heard of some taxi drivers on night shifts hallucinating. Maybe, hopefully, that was what was happening to him.

His heart was still beating fast from the scare inside the tunnel. He wanted to laugh at all this because who would believe him if he told someone he saw a fox spirit? Also, this was 2018; if he didn't take a picture, it didn't happen. Once he stopped his van he would take pictures, maybe then he would be able to assure himself that it was just a fox.

He headed toward the zoo and kept the radio on to occupy his mind. He didn't know what to think. His stomach was growling—he hadn't even had dinner yet. Maybe he would stop by his parents' apartment for some home-cooked meals instead of returning to his place with nothing but instant noodles in his pantry. Many restaurants would be closed by now because of the typhoon. He wanted to have something to look forward to, so he could take his mind off this weird fox.

The typhoon update came on: the storm would be making its landfall in less than an hour and the warning had been raised to level three. And this just in: a thirty-three year old man reported being followed and nearly attacked by a fox in the Happy Valley area half an hour ago. The victim managed to get away after a few stray dogs attacked the fox.

Jacky eyed the suspicious animal in his backseat, and tried to control his shaky hands on the steering wheel. What was the possibility of another fox roaming free in Hong Kong right where he had been earlier?

He pulled up to the parking lot of the zoo. There was nobody there now; the lights were dimmed since the zoo was closed. He parked his car and turned off the engine. It wasn't pitch black but dark enough that the fox was glowing red again. Jacky fumbled for his phone and tried to take a picture of it; the flash made the glow disappear. He disabled the flash, but it was so dark even the glowing redness didn't show the fox clearly and looked far too blurry to be believable.

"Oh, what the hell am I doing?" he said.

Realizing he had some messed up priorities, he called 999 and reached the police. He told them that he had the fox responsible for the previous attack and gave them his location. They would be there in half an hour, they said. They didn't seem too concerned because Jacky said the animal was listless or dying, but he couldn't tell them anything else (not the glowing red part certainly) because he didn't want it to sound like a prank, or that he was crazy.

The police's attitude was exactly what he feared—they didn't consider this a priority. He needed to find someone who could help him right now. He searched for the general number for the zoo and called, but nobody was answering. He looked for the Amazing Asian Animals department and was put on hold once he got through, since it was after hours and there were few staff sticking around in this weather. He was surprised he could reach anyone at all.

He kept glancing in the rear-view mirror. The fox was stirring now, the eight tails coming out from under the blanket. Jacky was beyond frightened; he had the urge to just leave the fox in the van and run off, hoping it was still too injured to attack him.

He ran through all the available options and possible plans quickly in his head. He could lock his car and wait for help outside, but what would he tell the police when they got there? Would he tell them what he thought the fox really was? What was it exactly?

He could call the Department of Agriculture, Fisheries and Conservation and tell them what he had told the police. Just like at the zoo, they would take the fox in and try to save it. But should he warn them what it really was? Would they believe him? What if he was the only one who could see its true form? Or was he losing his mind and imagining the whole thing?

He could ditch it. Throw the fox to the side of the road and leave it. But what if it healed itself and attacked, or even killed someone? It had already tried before, it would be morally reprehensible to let it roam free and attack again. He would be even worse than those idiots who kept exotic animals as pets and then abandoned them when they tore up their homes.

Of course, there was always the last resort. He could kill the thing—it had not attained immortality yet (as far as the legend went) with only eight tails. Right? But as a Buddhist and vegetarian, taking a life was against his core beliefs, despite Buddhist and Daoist monks killing demons and malevolent spirits in fiction. Would taking the life of a fox spirit in real life count as a sin?

Right now, even he thought he was going crazy!

He wondered if the attack victim earlier had seen the multiple tails or the red glow. Perhaps the guy didn't tell the cops everything for fear that they would think he was making it up or that *he* was crazy. Or maybe it was lit up where the fox tried to attack the guy so it wasn't glowing red or showing its eight tails. And did the light simply obscure the fox spirit's true form, whereas the darkness revealed it? This wasn't brought up in any of the soap operas! And what were the fox spirits afraid of?

"Hello, sir? This is Kitty at Amazing Asian Animals. Are you still there?" Finally there was a live person on the other line.

What to do? Jacky was torn. He wanted to do the right thing, or he wouldn't have rescued the fox in the first place. Maybe he could just get through the door, drop off the fox, get it contained, and then show them what it really was in the dark? Providing that he wasn't imagining the red glow and eight tails, of course. Then at least he wouldn't have to deal with the fox spirit alone. That sounded much better than all the other options.

"Yes! I found a fox on the side of the road and I don't know where to bring him. He's hurt badly but still alive," Jacky said. It wasn't a lie, but somehow he felt very guilty, like he was trying to deceive someone...not that different from what the fox spirit might do.

"Oh! It might be the same one that attacked someone earlier. You know what? Bring it in, we will keep it here for now," Kitty said. "Go south toward the cable car terminal and then follow the path to the Giant Panda Adventure, Amazing Asian Animals is right next to it. You can't miss it."

"All the gates must be locked by now, how do I get inside the park without paying?"

"I will have all the gates unlocked, no worries. Just proceed to our area and I will get you from there."

Sounded like a plan. Jacky was relieved for once; he wasn't alone in this anymore. All he had to do now was survive a two-minute drive down to Amazing Asian Animals. He could do this. A happy ending at last! Jacky broke into a huge grin at the thought. But when he looked at the rear-view mirror again, he dropped his phone.

The glowing red, eight-tailed fox was no longer wrapped up in the blanket, but was now right behind Jacky!

The musky scent in the car was intense. The fox had glowing red eyes, its mouth open and fangs protruding, ready to bite. The eight tails were fluffing up behind its head, fanning the odour all over the minivan. It made Jacky feel a bit woozy. He had remembered something about the fox spirits having a hard time hiding two of their tell-tale signs—their scent and their tails; even when disguised as humans, they could not hide them, not even with their dark magic. In TV shows and movies, it's almost always one of these two traits that give them away, even after they've shapeshifted into beautiful women. And that smell! He had been made fun of as a child because his last name Wu was homophonous with the word *fox* in Cantonese, which was the basis for the Cantonese slang "stinky fox", which meant someone with bad body odor. Now he knew why that term existed.

Jacky prided himself to be a manly man all these decades, but he nearly soiled himself seeing the fox like that. He panicked (who wouldn't?) and screamed, but the pouring rain outside was loud and nobody would hear him, especially not in an empty parking lot. He couldn't see where his phone had fallen. If it fell into the gap between his seat and the gear shift, he would not be able to reach it while fending off the fox.

He tried to open the car door but couldn't. The handle appeared to be stuck. He crawled to the passenger's side and it was the same. If the legend of the fox spirits held true, he's practically dead meat. You are what you eat, and if the fox had eaten someone who knew how to drive, it would know how to use or disable the various mechanisms in a car. He could only hope the fox didn't eat someone really smart and tech savvy. But what could he do now? He couldn't just give into passive wishful thinking and depend on luck that the fox would not devour him.

He grasped for anything that would help, but realized he had nothing. He fumbled to turn the lights on, and the glowing red fox turned back to a regular fox. Did that mean light was his only defense?

He looked at the fox and held his breath, not sure whether he would be mauled by the demonic spirit or the regular fox. Neither outcome was acceptable.

The fox saw where Jacky turned the lights on and flicked the switch off, turning the car into a dark box. It was glowing red again, its eyes angry and hungry, and they centered on Jacky's chest. Jacky wanted to turn away but couldn't. He was mesmerized, even though the fox did not shapeshift into a beautiful woman like he kept hoping. The musky scent of the fox obfuscated him. The fox had one paw up, inching it closer and closer to Jacky's chest, its claws sharp and long, ready to rip into his flesh, which was only protected by the thin fabric of a cheap short-sleeve tee-shirt his mother had bought him from Mong Kok.

Jacky's phone rang. It snapped him out of his mental fog and he saw that the fox's claws had ripped his tee-shirt open, drawing blood from his flesh. He felt a sting, shrieked and tried to turn the light on, but the switch did not work. When the fox's eyes bore into his, he could see wisdom in them—the fox had clued in on the light source and had probably used magic to disable it. He reached down to grab his phone, which he could now see was under the brake, but couldn't answer it in time. The call was probably from Kitty, wondering why he had not shown up yet. He managed to use the flashlight function on his phone, which the fox hadn't clued in on yet. When the light turned on, the fox immediately backed off.

"Ha!" Jacky screamed in victory, however short-lived that might be. The fox might change back to its regular form, but it was still a wild animal that could kill him in the car. He had completely been trapped, being unable to open the car doors to escape. He was bleeding superficially from the chest where the fox had torn his shirt open. The metallic smell of his blood drew the fox closer and closer. The flashlight from his phone would eventually go out as the battery ran low (right now it was at 33%). Out of sheer frustration and fear, he sounded the horn, long and hard, before the fox disabled that too.

Jacky opened his glove compartment and took out a flashlight, but the fox swiped it from his hand, leaving his fingers bleeding from multiple cuts. Jacky screamed in pain. The fox drew nearer to him, tasting victory now that he was bleeding from both his chest and fingers. Jacky took out the car manual he had never read and hit the fox with it. He used it as a shield as the fox started to gnaw at him left and right, though occasionally moaning in pain from its injury.

Wait!

It suddenly dawned on Jacky what the fox's weakness might be. The news said that the attack was foiled when the fox was attacked by stray dogs. That's it! In Japanese folklore the fox spirits were afraid of dogs—especially their barks—because a dog's bark would turn the fox spirit back into its original form if it had shapeshifted into something else. Oh, how he regretted shooing away those two stray dogs when he first found the fox.

He suddenly felt a sting across his face. The fox had clawed him right on his left cheek and left a gash. He tasted blood dripping from his cheek into his mouth. He screamed in agony while still using his tattered car manual to shield himself from further attacks. It wouldn't hold forever, he needed to act quickly. He fumbled to grab the phone which had fallen on the passenger's seat and turned it on. He opened his internet browser and searched for dog barking videos, and clicked on one that was five minutes long.

The sound of the dog barking forced the fox to retreat all the way to the back of the minivan. Jacky seized the opportunity to try to open his car door. To his immense relief and surprise, it opened! He turned the lights on inside the car for good measure. A few tears fell from his eyes to join the pouring rain outside as he made a mad dash toward the zoo.

Jacky left his cell phone in the car to buy himself five minutes to escape. Everything was computer controlled nowadays. The lock on the gate was disabled and he could get into the zoo without someone physically there to unlock it. He ran past the cable car terminal, and from there he followed the signs pointing to the Giant Panda Adventure. He hadn't been to the zoo for many years—he had no real reason to, as he had no kids or nieces and nephews to take to it. He was the only child, and his cousins had left Hong Kong before the Chinese takeover in 1997, so he had only his parents in his family. He thought of his parents as he kept on running. He couldn't imagine them losing their only child in their old age. Parents should not have to bury their children.

Once he saw the big statue of the giant panda, he saw a sign pointing to Amazing Asian Animals and ran toward it. He was completely drenched and bleeding from the face, chest and fingers. The rain was blurring out his vision but he could still make out a figure standing at the entrance.

Jacky was never so happy to see a complete stranger. And this stranger happened to be a stunningly beautiful woman with pale skin, round eyes, a small, straight nose, plump pink lips and long dark hair past her shoulders. He couldn't tell her age—she seemed like the timeless beauty type—but she had to be younger than forty. She stood there holding an umbrella, but the wind was strong and she was getting wet nonetheless.

"Hi, I'm Kitty. Are you okay? Where is the fox?" she asked, looking very concerned at all the blood running down Jacky's face, fingers and chest.

"It attacked me. I had to escape. It's still in my minivan in the parking lot," Jacky found himself panting and yelling his answers over the howling storm.

"Come on in, let's get you dried and fixed up," Kitty said.

They stepped inside. He could smell the animals in there, musky and pungent. His eyes couldn't help but linger on her behind; she definitely had the right curves: her buttocks were full, not flat...he had to snap himself out of his fantasy as he followed her.

She led Jacky directly to the "Employees Only" area, a small room that had a few lockers, cabinetry, a sink, fridge, microwave, table and a few chairs. She opened a cabinet and took out a towel and handed it to Jacky. He was so relieved that he cried as he told the woman the whole story, nearly mesmerized when she looked at him with her large round eyes beneath those long eyelashes, her glossy black hair cascading down one side as she tilted her head to listen to his story. She was simply too beautiful, too perfect.

Kitty got up to get a soda from the fridge. Her full buttocks looked bigger than before and were jiggling now. It looked like something was about to come out of them, and Jacky soon figured out what. It was always one, if not both, of the traits that gave the fox spirits away.

When he turned around and tried to leave the room, his feet accidentally kicked something under his chair. It was a cracked cell phone. There was also a handbag with its contents spilling out of it under the table. There were drops of blood around it too.

"Goddess of Mercy!" Jacky exclaimed, realizing what might have happened here, but it was too late. The lights suddenly went out, and in the room with him was a glowing red fox with eight tails.

Jacky screamed when "Kitty" the fox charged at him. Its claws dug into his chest and ripped out his heart. The fox shoved the heart into its mouth and swallowed it whole. Jacky's expression was frozen with his eyes bugged out and mouth agape. The fox crunched Jacky's head like it was iceberg lettuce and went on to devour the entire body; the clothes were torn anyway; it could conjure up new ones. It left nothing behind but blood splatter. It licked the blood clean, relishing every drop.

Kitty walked toward the parking lot, where she spotted the police flashing their emergency lights. The rain had lessened a bit now, but she was wet nonetheless.

There were two police cruisers parked next to Jacky's minivan. She approached them.

"Are you Mr. Jacky Wu? Is this your vehicle?" a uniformed officer asked. The lights inside the minivan were still on just as Jacky had left them. "May I see your licence and registration please?"

"Yes, sir." Kitty reached into the glove compartment, took out the driver's licence and vehicle registration and handed them to the police, who all had their guns at the ready.

The enquiring officer examined Jacky's driver's licence with his flashlight and looked up at Kitty. He used his phone and took a picture of the licence and vehicle registration before giving them back to her.

"Mr. Wu, the fox is dead; we will have to hand the body over to Conservation and Fisheries to dispose of it. They are closed right now so we will keep the dead fox in the morgue. They might run some tests on it to see if it carried any diseases and try to find out how it even showed up in Hong Kong. We were just waiting for you to return so we could take the fox from your vehicle," the officer said. "I gotta warn you though, it's really stinky here because of the dead fox. You may want to disinfect your whole interior."

The car keys were still in the ignition.

"We figured you must have taken off because of the stench without even taking your keys with ya," another officer said.

"Phew! I hope you can get the smell out!" the third cop said.

"We can take your statements now or you can come by the station tomorrow, if you wish. You might want to head home if you want to avoid the storm," the first officer said.

With Kitty's permission, the three cops opened her car doors and used gloves to handle the dead fox's body. They moved it into one of the cruisers' trunks. It had a very strong stench, a mixture of death and musky wildlife scent.

Pity, you were so close, thought Kitty. She bade the officers goodbye and promised to give a statement the next day.

Kitty started the car. When she looked in the visor mirror the reflection was not the beautiful woman she was before, but an older man with wrinkles and sun damage on his face. It was Jacky's face. At least her tail hid very well on this bigger, fatter body. She was going to Jacky's parents' home. That was in his heart and thankfully, she learned how to drive through him too. A few more and she would be immortal. If the cops didn't have guns she would have finished them right there and then, but alas, it was just a small delay. Soon, she wouldn't have to put up with these stupid humans anymore!

She drove off toward the Aberdeen Tunnel. As she turned the interior lights off, her true form revealed in the darkness: a soon-to-be nine-tailed fox.

CHILD OF THE EARTH: A TALE OF THE BAJAZID
Kenneth Bykerk

"Goddamn! What the fuck is that?"

Yesil Batur snapped his hand back from the table, a look of absolute disgust on his face. An abomination an inch long had made its presence known when Yesil reached for his coffee. Now, standing a good safe step back from the table, he glared at his abandoned cup with dismay as the thing that looked like a cricket reformed in the pits of Hell crawled beneath the cover of the cup's curvature.

"¿Jefe? Oh...", Hector Montalvo, foreman, peered at the table and then crossed himself.

"What was that? Why the fuck did you do that? What is that thing?"

"That thing, Señor Batur, is el niño de la tierra."

"Child of the earth? What the hell does that mean? Does it bite?"

"I don't know, Señor Batur. I just know that it is bad and that it cries like a baby."

"Cries like a baby?"

"Si, Señor, and if you hear its cries, it means something bad is happening somewhere."

"Bok! That don't mean nothing. Bad shit's always happening somewhere."

"Cerca."

"Still, superstitious hogwash." Yesil had been examining the freak of nature from his distance but slowly closing in as interest overcame disgust. "Damn, that is one ugly cricket. It's a cricket, right?"

"No lo sé, Señor."

"Do you know anything about it? I mean, does it sting or anything?"

"I just know they are malos presagios, ill omens, Señor."

89

"Then what good are you?" Yesil was bent low, his face a foot away from his cup and the creature hiding beneath. It was a loathsome thing, a putrid ochre with black bands striping its abdomen. The thought of what would happen if a cricket fucked an ant crossed Yesil's mind. The body lay close to the table, its legs crouched like an ant unable to support itself. The head too resembled that of an ant in shape, an elongated oval, but with marked differences. The antenna projected forth from just forward the eyes and those eyes were not distinct from the head about them but visible still beneath the translucent shell covering it. The apparatus of its mouth and the large, black mandibles forming from beneath the eyes gave it the vague affection of a skull. "Why are you here?"

"Señor, the men, they have found something. They, how you say, break through, una gran cueva, a big cave, Señor."

"What?"

"They broke through, Señor. The men, they were drilling and the wall came down and…"

"The wall came down? Anyone injured?"

"No, Señor. Todos son buenos, Señor."

Yesil shrugged and picked up his coffee cup. The perversion that had sought shelter beneath began crawling, seeking new cover. "Well, what of this big cave? Get to the point."

"Si, Señor. The wall, it came down, colapsado…"

"Yes, yes…it came down. What about it."

"Señor, there is a big cave. It is grande, enorme and the men, they are afraid."

"Afraid? What? Is any work being done?"

"Si, jefe, the other crews are working still. It is just this one crew. They broke through and they don't know what to do. I do not know what to do. That is why I came for you, jefe. This is un gran discumbrimiento, Señor."

"Very well, let's go."

With that, Yesil drained his coffee and slammed the cup down hard on the ugly thing crawling across the table.

The Mortenson Mine was founded in 1867 when a company of men prospecting in the Silver Mountains for gold struck it rich beyond their wildest dreams on a creek they christened the Bajazid. Over the corpse of one of their own, a luckless lad named Isaiah Baird, the mine had started at the tip of a granite outcrop over the creek from which the young man had slipped and fallen upon spying an open vein glistening in the sun. The original production had cut direct into that outcrop, continuing until the entire shoulder of land had been sheered a hundred and fifty yards back to the rise of the mountain proper. The whole of the hill had been cleared, tons of earth extracted and ran through a ten-stamp mill built over the edge of the stream. Over time, the hill that had been removed reformed below that mill, forcing the creek to seek a course around as the dam gave birth to a small, dirty lake. Upstream, barely a quarter mile distant, the town of Baird's Holler rose and fell, the whole of the population left but three ignorant to the origins of that name.

Now, twenty-three years later, Baird's Holler was but a hollow shell of the glory it once had attained. Gone were the hotels and saloons, the churches and neighborhoods which had risen in the boom of prosperity. Fire had razed the town twice in its time and what remained was but a fraction of what was. Along with the demise of the town, the Mortenson Mine had begun to wither and die. There remained gold abundant within that mountain; the veins were never shy about revealing themselves. That was not the problem. The death of the mine came from rumor and fear, a millstone which hung about the valley whole. A reputation had grown, one which the owners of the mine were at a loss about how to dismiss. It was this reputation, that the town and the mine itself were cursed, which had reduced dramatically the number of those willing to enter the heart of that mountain. After the second fire three years prior, the remaining population collapsed leaving but a ghost lingering and those who stayed were the meanest and most desperate, desperate enough to descend where no others dared.

The offices of the Mortenson Mine were two hundred yards from where the complete removal of earth gave way to a reinforced adit fixed with strengthened double-doors hanging open. A solitary, weathered shack sat by the opening where a guard was posted during the day. This had once been a great and prosperous mine, one where such precautions as had been taken in support and fortification had been needed. Now that entrance was devoid of life, except when crews came and went, but for the guard that kept an eye on the stores of old rail and other equipment haphazardly strewn about the yard. The guard was no longer needed to keep people out, though that remained the pretense for keeping one, for there were none to protect the mine against. The citizens of Baird's Holler, those not directly associated with the work of the mine, kept their distance for each their own reasons. The guards were there to keep some of the men who worked the mines working; not all who went below did so willingly. Along with the desperate and damned, two populations, neither fluent in English, entered each morning and left each night under armed guard, marched to and from barracks built between the town and mine.

Once upon a time, this, labor forced on the end of a chain, would have disgusted Yesil Batur. Once he would have denounced such as slavery. In his foolish youth, before a true meaning glistened in his world, he had taken up the Abolitionist cause, its rhetoric sweeping him knowingly into the final days of a brutal conflict. He was just eighteen and eager to prove himself, for short was his stature and slight his build. A soldier though knows no distinction in size when the *Minié* balls are blind. If anything, Yesil had thought he would provide a smaller target. He never got a chance to test out that theory for a peace was signed in a place called Appomattox before he even made it to Virginia. The war was over and within two years, having traveled in the wake of the western diaspora, Yesil found himself wealthy beyond all imagining as one of that party, who had come to be called the Sultans, those who had found that gold glistening in that stream. Years and priorities take their toll on foolish ideals. What he once condemned as slavery he saw now as necessity. It was Yesil who had proposed the barracks following the last burning, one for the Chinese and one for the Mexicans whose labor they had need for. The third barracks were for the damned, those others free to come and go as they pleased but whose desperation left them no choice but digging in Hell for another's purse.

It was only two hundred yards but it was a most dreaded walk. Yesil did not like entering the mine. This he would tell himself and the only other remaining Sultan whose interest in the mine mattered, Thomas Lundmeir. Tom, for his part, held similar sentiments, confessions admitted under covers after they became the sole active owners two years prior. Three other Sultans remained beyond Yesil and Tom, their interests in the mine now but numbers changing in a bank ledger. Two were absent but the third, the third was standing amidst a group of men gathered at the adit. Seeing the Colonel anywhere near the mine helped fuel the smoldering indignation burning in Yesil at having to even come this close to the entrance. He and Tom had foremen for that.

The last few yards, burning hot with annoyance, Yesil snapped at Hector, "I thought you said they were working?"

"Sí, Señor, they were."

"Which crew did you say found this cave? Yours?"

"Sí."

"You boss the greasers, evet?"

"Eh? Si! Yes, yes I do."

"Then where the fuck are your boys and why the hell are...Arliss!" Nearing, Yesil raised his voice to the assembled crowd, "Arliss, why the hell ain't your boys working? I ain't paying them to stand around!"

The man hailed stepped forth from the dozen milling at the adit as Yesil closed the gap. "Sir, there's been a..."

"There's been a breakthrough or something, yes. Why are you out here? Your crew didn't find it, did they?"

"No, but..."

"Then why the fuck are you standing around out here?" Yesil at last acknowledged his fellow Sultan with a glare and a curt nod, "William."

"Yesil." The Colonel, William Nesmith, returned the nod, a thin smile hiding behind a thick brush of fast greying beard.

"Cut the shit. What are you doing here?"

"I still retain stake and share in this mine, Yesil. Need I remind you of that?"

"Need I remind you I have documents in my possession which you signed relinquishing you of all managerial responsibilities?" Yes, Yesil was prickly this morning. His coffee had gotten cold waiting and his head still wasn't square from the previous night's debauch. Yesil had left Tom asleep, sprawled in an opium dream next to the whore they'd favored these last few months.

"Pish-posh! I ain't here to take nothin' from you. I'm just curious is all." There was a deep Southern drawl in the Colonel's speech.

"Curious? How the hell? What do you know? How do you know?"

"Everyone knows. I'm just the only one ain't too yeller to come see what's what." William gestured behind Yesil, up past the office and past the triple barracks and beyond the wooden bridge to the westernmost edge of town. There, dozens of people stood on the bank of the creek or crowded further up on the boardwalk before Barons, one of the two remaining saloons in Baird's Holler.

"What the hell? How come everyone knows something's up but me? Hector! Why didn't you come get me?" Frustration fueled by confusion turned the question into a bitter accusation.

"I looked for you, Señor Batur. I looked everywhere for you."

"Bullshit!"

"I did! Me and Juan, we…"

"Did you look in the privy?"

"Señor?"

"Did you bother to fucking check the goddamn privy?" Yesil was screaming, his face red. He knew why they couldn't find him and their excuse was legitimate. He had been gone for some time sitting in the outhouse reading a month-old copy of the Weekly Journal Miner out of Prescott. He loved his opium, he truly did, but he also knew it was the cause of his bowel trouble. Try as he might, each morning after he'd smoked the dream pipe, this same story repeated itself. He'd been feeling quite satisfied when he stepped back into the office, quite satisfied indeed only to see Hector waiting for him. Now he had to bluster past embarrassment and Yesil had grown cruel in the years of his dominance. Hector, for his part, stood with mouth gaping, a dumb, confused look on his face. "Well?"

"I'm sorry, Señor. I will revisa la letrina, Señor Batur." Hector's eyes were cast down, examining the dirt as he twisted his cap in hand.

Some veins are fool's missions to chase and Yesil realized this was one. "No hay problema, olvídalo." Then, with a very unconvincing smile, "No soy un dios, Hector. Yo cago igual que tú." Can't afford to scare off one of the few men he trusted.

Hector's laugh was just as unconvincing. He was disturbed and it showed. "Sí, Señor, you shit too."

Fighting the urge to snap again at Hector, Yesil breathed deep before speaking. "Okay, now that we've established I shit like everyone else, can anyone of you bastards tell me what the fuck is going on here?"

Hector raised his eyes at last to Yesil's. "I told you, jefe, we broke through to una gran cueva."

"Yes, now what about it has all these men standing around gawking on my time? You men are on the clock. Why ain't you working? It was the greaser crew, not you, am I right?"

Several of the men gathered mumbled and averted their eyes.

"And if you're up here, then who's running your crew, Hector? Juan?"

"No, Señor, I sent Juan to your casa to get you."

"You what? Fuck! Fuck!" This was not good. Tom was apt to wake mean on mornings after dreaming with the pipe, and now, all because Yesil had clogged up his, it was all but guaranteed. His morning repast was going to echo all up the canyon by the end of the day. "And who's watching your crew?"

"Jorge…"

"Who? Fuck! Never mind. Well, tell me about this big cave of yours then."

"You must see to believe it, Señor Batur."

"He's right, sir. I went down there to take a look-see for myself and I ain't got no words to say. It ain't somethin' words can describe." The men around began nodding and muttering agreements with Arliss.

"What the hell? Is everyone crazy today? What do you mean you don't have words to describe it? It's a cave, ain't it?"

"Yes sir, but it's…" Arliss shrugged his shoulders. "I can't say. It ain't nothin' I seen the likes of before."

Yesil was realizing, to his deep dread and distaste, that he was going to have to go into the mine this morning. He was hoping to forestall the trip, learn what he could so that he could issue edicts from the comfort of being anywhere but in that mine. Interrogation though was proving fruitless. He was surrounded by idiots.

"Jefe …"

With great patience, "Yes, Hector?"

Hector raised his arm, one finger pointing to Yesil's left shoulder.

95

"Oh, look at that!" There was more excitement in William's voice than was necessary, at least until Yesil caught sight of what William reached forth and plucked off his jacket. It was another of those damned crickets from Hell, right there, crawling on his shoulder and now it was pinched in William Nesmith's fingers as the Colonel examined it closely. "Wó see ts'inii."

Horror was plain and clear on Yesil's face as he glared at the bug struggling between William's pinched fingers. That thing had been crawling on him and William, who he'd already known was crazy, was holding it before his face in close examination. Incredulity left him only one word, "What?"

"Navajo. That's what the Navajo call these things. It means skull-face bug."

Yesil just stared at William, disbelief on his face. "And when did you start speaking Navajo?"

"Yii yaa xaa bááhádzid."

"Goddamn and fuck you, Nesmith! Just go to Hell!"

If there was any single phrase Yesil would have preferred not to hear at this moment of all moments, it was that. It hearkened back, this phrase, to the day their party, the Mortenson Company, came into this valley and first found the stream with gold lying open for the taking. Those were the words their guide, a native hired to lead them safely through the mountains, shouted in warning as he fled into the brush upon recognizing the creek. That first night, as the Mortenson men reveled in their newfound wealth and argued over possible names for the creek, Yesil mentioned into the din that the word spoken by their late guide was similar in sound to the name of a great Sultan from the antiquity of his native lands. The name was adopted immediately, the spelling determined later by chance.

"I already am, Yesil, and so are you." William replied.

"You don't know for sure that was what he said."

"Yes, yes I do and you know it as well. We're just waiting for our turns, that's all."

"Horseshit!"

"Where are all the others then?"

"You know as good as I do where they are. They're dead, which is what happens to all of us. They're dead or they've moved away like Chesterfield and Kearns."

"Kearns is still here. You think he's escaped? Pitt's Junction is on the Sultana, Yesil, and the Sultana, as you know, feeds the Bajazid. And what about Alexander? Where is he?"

This sent a chill down Yesil's spine. Two years prior, another Sultan, Alexander Gitney, disappeared from his house without a trace after leaving a will signed on his writing table. The will stipulated that Yesil and Tom receive all his interest in future mining profits as well as "all damnations therein". Yesil glared at William and growled, "You know where he is. He spent his last day jawin' it up with you. Had himself a nice dinner, went home and wrote his will. What was your hand in that? Was that damnation joke yours?"

William laughed, an unexpected burst into the tense air. "Ha! I forgot about that! No, I didn't have anything to do with that. Why don't you ask him? You're goin' in the mine, ain't you?"

Yesil wanted more than anything to kill William Nesmith at that moment. His hand had even drifted of its own to his belt. There was a long-standing hatred between these two men. With over two dozen sharing ownership in the mine, John S. Mortenson, the man who financed and led the expedition which cemented their fortunes, had built into the contract each man signed traps preventing the members from taking advantage of each other, particularly through means nefarious. As time passed, Sultans died one by one either through tragedy or illness but only once through murder by another Sultan. Greed dwells deep and powerful on the Bajazid, but the traps left by Mortenson had done their job. Instead of blood feuds, as divisions tore the Sultans apart over the years, it was through forced politeness and deadly glares they waged their wars.

The rest of those assembled stared at the two Sultans, oblivious to the private implications of the conversation shared. Of those overt, that there was something about the mine which these two men spoke well around they all heeded and heard what wasn't said. They all had heard the stories of men who had gone missing in the mines and who would turn up later, walking dead men covered in fungal growths. Other stories of hauntings and things unexplained, all lurid and suspicious in the eyes of rational men, added to the specter that haunted the valley. The eyes of rational men though are blind to what they cannot account. They dismiss what they refuse to see.

"I swear to God, Bill, you keep this up and there will be trouble."

"There is already trouble, and you know it. Now, what are you going to do with your precious mine? You're the boss. I'm here to help anyway I can, upon my word. Just tell me what you need."

"How about you get the hell out of here and go back to your dolls?" Then, eying the sack slung over the Colonel's shoulder, "You ain't got any of them here with you, do you?"

The Colonel simply shrugged, his smile still unchanged, and flicked the ugly little bug from his fingers. It landed on one of the miners gathered around, a big man whose reaction to having this thing land on his chest was explosive. William Nesmith was a known quantity in Baird's Holler. He was protected both by his status as a Sultan as well the reputation which had grown around this thin, aging man wearing worn, unkempt clothes. Still, slighted, the giant pushed his way past those before him with vengeance on his lips. He drew up quick as William, fast as lightening, cocked a Colt Navy in the man's face. With his other hand, William drew from the sack a small doll, a hand-sewn rag recognizable enough with two small buttons on the misshapen head for eyes, and tossed it to the feet of the big man.

The effect of this doll landing in the dirt was instant. Everyone but Yesil took a step back. Yesil just rolled his eyes.

"Goddamnit, William, will you put that fucking thing away?"

"Here's a doll for you," William drawled soft and slow, his flat, steady gaze leveled on the slack-jawed giant.

"Fuck! Damnit! William, you're not helping!"

Holstering his pistol, the big man dismissed, William drawled, "Well, you ain't told us what you're gonna do. Shall we wait for Tom?"

This decided Yesil. He and Tom had been running the mine exclusively for two years without the input of any others. Things had been going good, or as good as they could. The output from the mine was minimal due to both labor shortages as well as the increased isolation of Baird's Holler, but gold still poured forth. This was his kingdom and Yesil was determined to rule it as he saw fit. The only challenge to his authority was

Tom Lundmeir and Tom had a temper. Not that Yesil didn't, but he preferred to not be on the receiving end of Tom's.

"What I want is for you to leave but since you won't, keep your mouth shut about your damned dolls. For God's sake, don't rile 'em up."

"On my word, Yesil. I'll wait out here and keep the natives pacified until Tom arrives. He should be waking up sometime before noon, shouldn't he?"

"Shut up." Turning from the Colonel, Yesil swept up the gaping horde with his eyes. "Ya'll come with me. Get yourselves some picks. We're gonna go see what the greasers have found. If they're shammin', if we have trouble, I want you men backing me up. You'll get paid, don't worry. Bolton, any more guns in the shack?"

"Yes, Mr. Batur. Got about six in there."

"Get them. You…you…you and you. You're getting shotguns. Hector and Arliss, you too. The rest of you, grab some picks. If we have trouble, you guys get to have some fun. Just remember, you don't go beating on them until I give the say-so. Understand?"

The men about all nodded, smiles forming on their dirty faces. Desperate men desire nothing more than to see another put beneath them. This was a truth Yesil well knew. Grant a bum the chance to stand tall over another, give them the illusion of power, and they were in for a penny. Promise them a dollar, and their greed enslaves. Letting these men stand tall in the shadow of his gold for loyalty was worth at least a dollar promised.

"Good, now get moving. Arliss, one moment…"

Everyone but Arliss scrambled, anticipation of a brawl spurring their heels.

"Yes, boss?"

"I want to know where the rest of your men are and why the hell they ain't working."

"Sir?"

"Don't sir me! This was Hector's crew. You're down D-line, right? Hector's crew is on H, right?"

"Well yes…"

"So why are you up here and not down there on D-line?"

"We heard…"

"How? How did you hear?"

"Rocky, Rocky met Hector coming back. Hector told him."

"So that meant you dropped your work?"

"Well, we were curious. Sorry boss, but the boys wanted to take a look-see."

"You will be sorry, believe me, if this is less than spectacular."

"Oh, it is spectacular, sir! Honest!"

Yesil glared at him. His own extended absence still hanging over him, he couldn't very well come down too hard on Arliss lest he need his support in the mine. If this turned out to be nothing though, Yesil determined Arliss would no longer be supervising anything and might very well work well on one of the other crews. That brought forth another thought, one he'd failed to probe to this point.

"Where are the coolies? They still on E-line?"

"As far as I know, boss."

"Damnit, find out! No, send one of your boys down and tell Heng to bring them out. I want them back in the barracks in case there's trouble."

"Yes, sir, right away."

Arliss turned on his heel and started running after the men heading into the mine. Yesil smiled. That was how things were supposed to work. Immediate and complete obedience. That left the problem at hand, the issue of this grand cave. Of course, that meant entering the mine. Yesil bowed his head and shook it. Even if all this was for nothing, he was still having to go into the mine. Never before had he wished he'd stayed in the privy longer, but this day, he did.

"Good luck in there, Yesil. I mean that."

"Sure you do, Bill, sure you do." With that, Yesil sighed and set his steps to the mine. He so wished William hadn't reminded him of what their guide had said.

The Mortenson Mine spun an array of tunnels in a web from the main line which ran a twisting path hundreds of feet deep into the mountain. Rich ore deposits had been chased on a relatively horizontal plane resulting in the need for very few shafts. Instead, a web of crosscuts connected the seven drift tunnels which ran off of the A-line. Smaller drifts chased feeders off each of these resulting in a maze of over sixty miles carefully diagramed on a large map in the mine's offices. The A-line had been long established, widened and strengthened to support the loads of the whole mine transported through it. Some of the secondary tunnels had played out, or seemingly so while others had simply been abandoned in the pursuit of richer veins. Only three were currently being worked and the H-line, the deepest and newest branch, was where the discovery had been made.

The H-line was barely a year old and the only time Yesil had ever been down this far was when he and Tom did an initial inspection upon discovery. It took twenty minutes of walking through the dark of the A-line just to reach the junction where the H-line diverged. He loathed having to go into the mine at all, let alone this deep. He hadn't any true reason to loathe the mine. He was not one to believe in ghosts or haunts or the other tales he'd heard these many years. That was all fancy from the minds of the weak. Hell, he could even properly place blame for most of the superstitious nonsense and he did. When he straightened out this mess, he'd determined he'd take care of Colonel William Nesmith once and for all. Until then, he had to put on his bravest face for the men in his train and that fouled his mood with each step.

The H-line was narrow. Newly begun and worked with coerced labor poorly supervised, it hadn't been widened more than five feet, just enough for rails to be laid through its center. They had to travel two abreast, ten men trailing Yesil, with oil-wick lamps bobbing on their helmets and a few lanterns swinging in stride. Yesil had never been down the H-line before and noted with professional disgust the shoddy engineering which had gone into the excavation and support. He would have to speak to Hector about that. He was going to have a very good talk with Hector about quite a few things as soon as this got resolved. Perhaps he'd bust Hector down to the greaser crew. That'd show him, that'd teach that...

And when something moves around one's neck beneath the collar, something moving with intent, that disturbs even the most focused thought. Muttering a curse, Yesil slapped at his neck with his free hand. There! He felt it. He swatted again, this time pinioning the creature crawling under his collar. Pinching the wiggling thing in his fingers, he pulled it forth to the lantern in his other hand.

101

"Fuck!"

"What is it, boss?" Arliss stepped even to peer at Yesil's prize.

"It's another one of those ugly fucking bugs! Goddamnit! That fucking thing was on my neck! Why the fuck are they all over now? I ain't seen one 'til today and now they're all over me? Hector, don't you do that shit again! I don't care if you want to piss yourself in private, but don't you dare do that here!"

Hector had crossed himself and his expression in the flickering wicks of the assembled was of supernatural fear. "Señor, this is bad. Three niño de la tierra, Señor. ¡Tres!"

"Hogwash, Hector. Jerusalem crickets are harmless. Well, they got a bite, but they's harmless otherwise." Arliss drawled.

"So they are crickets?" Yesil could handle crickets.

"I think so, boss. There ain't nothin' special about them but ugly though. Knew someone who kept some as pets in a box."

Yesil looked disgusted at Arliss. How or why could anyone want one of these around he knew not. Thinking that, he dropped it to the dirt and squashed it with his foot.

"You want to make a pet of that, Arliss, you're gonna have to scrape it up. Hector, grow some balls, man! It's just a bug, for Christ's sake. Come on."

Not a step was taken when a low vibration of the air began to stir about them. It was a sound so low, so rapid and fluttering that it was impossible to tell its direction. Those in the tunnel looked at one another, curiosity and confusion on their faces. Questions were whispered amongst the men, queries as to whether any knew what this was. All were confounded as the thrumming rose, but only enough to make out distinct fluctuating rhythms and patterns competing for dominance. They stood there listening to this incessant buzz until a new sound made itself heard over the thrumming, the sound of men screaming in fear.

"Shit! Shit!" Someone behind Yesil started shouting.

"What? What?" Yesil thundered and turned to see the men in his crew begin swatting at themselves and yelping in alarm. It looked to Yesil as if everyone had gone mad. The frantic gesticulations, their dance of disgust sent the light from their lamps in chaotic display. Yesil caught short flashes of men flailing with faces drawn in dread. They were stark

102

shadows screaming like children. Yesil stared in disbelief at the display before him until he felt at once dozens of pairs of little legs crawling beneath his trousers as his collar came alive with the same sensation. This was the catalyst, the moment the world shifted beneath Yesil's feet. He joined his curses to the others for such caress was intolerable. Nearer too came the frantic cries, in English and in Spanish, from deeper down the H-line.

Fifteen yards distant, the tunnel took a hard turn. Yesil was facing that direction when the first fleeing miners came barreling down that passage, pushing and shoving at each other in their panic. When they saw Yesil and his men, they redoubled their cries to flee at those before them. Yesil, already hot, burst at seeing what he deemed immediately an insurrection, a strike. This is what he had come to counter. This was what he had come into this hole to do. Forgetting the things crawling beneath his clothes, he drew his pistol and shouted.

"Stop! ¡Detener! Stop, goddammit!"

The men running at him did not hear nor care. They were panic-blind, running and screaming in a fearsome rout. Blinded by his own rage, Yesil fired. The shot was deafening in the close confines of the tunnel. The shot was deadly to the man in the lead, a Mexican in dun tunic and trousers. He arched backwards, his face a torn blush, and was dragged down by those behind heedless of all but escape. Before Yesil could fire again, they were on him and pushing past. Yesil was pinned to the wall by the procession which tripped and stumbled over his own bought men.

As the last of a dozen men shoved themselves past, Yesil recognized one from Arliss' crew and blocked him, pistol jamming into the man's gut.

"What the fuck is going on? Where the fuck are you going?"

The man, his eyes rabid with fear, grabbed Yesil back and screamed in his face, "Run! Run, boss! Jesus Christ! Run!" Ignoring the pistol to his gut, the man tore the lantern from Yesil's grip. "Run! It's coming! It's coming!"

Stunned at the violence of his terror, Yesil watched astonished as the man took a couple running steps and hurled the lantern down the hallway. It exploded against the passage wall in a riot of flame. This was madness. Yesil watched as three men, stragglers, came running right through that wall of fire, the oil having splashed them when the lantern burst. They were burning but they kept running, screaming like demons from Hell. His promised guard had been knocked over like nine-pins and they were struggling for the composure of their feet while twitching in disgust at the little feet crawling over them. Yes - this was madness, and Yesil had but one law by which to gain control. He raised his revolver and put a bullet into the head of the man who had thrown the lantern. Then, half to assuage his rage and, to his immediate amusement, a flicker of pity, he shot the three burning men down one by one as they ran, the last falling at his feet.

Turning, he screamed at his men, "What the fuck is wrong with you? They walked right the fuck over you! What the Hell?"

"Boss, we gotta go! We gotta get out of here!" Arliss' beard was crawling with vermin.

"Yeah, and when we do, I'm gonna skin all of you but until I say we leave, we're gonna see this goddamn cave! Come on!"

Defiant determination had taken hold. Yesil took two steps down the hallway and stopped, head lowered, glowering. Primal passions slay the reasoned thought and fury consumes its remains. Fury had overcome Yesil. Never had he been so balked, so disparaged. His authority was questioned beyond what he could take. He had been lured down here to inspect something and damnit, he was going to know what was wrong with his mine.

"One of you is going to die right now if you don't start doing as I say." It was spoken in a low growl, one deep with threat amid the echoing screams before and behind. Yesil had no patience left. His anger and rage had reached an apoplectic end. He pulled back the hammer of his Colt, turned, and swung it slow between Hector and Arliss. "Well?"

"Boss..."

Arliss' tone held a note that begged Yesil's attention. The look on Arliss' face was definite. Yesil turned to see one more man staggering through the conflagration. His clothes had caught but he made no attempts to combat the flame. Over his visible flesh, illuminated by the flame that licked at and around him, a fluid mass of insects swarmed. From his lips, an anguished recitation made itself heard above the waning screams in either direction.

"...nosotros perdonamos a los que nos ofenden..."

104

As he spoke, a wave of russet-orange began to flow over the edges of the fire still burning in the tunnel, swarming and smothering in a blackening wave. The smoke from the sacrificed masses rose as a curtain behind him and the burning stench of their corpses preceded.

"…No nos dejes caer en tentación y líbranos del mal…"

On the word "Amen", as waves of insects extinguished themselves to flame, a beam shot from the veil of smoke and swept the doomed man's feet from beneath him. Upon striking the ground, the bugs crawling over him were scattered and Yesil saw, to his horror, the man's skull picked clean to the bone. And still he crawled, arms hanging in tatters, pulling himself along as the stench of the insects choked the passage.

Despite all they had witnessed, despite all the horror and nightmare they had just experienced, Yesil's men had held their ground. Through all of this they had maintained some semblance of humanity, the thin rational edge of their minds stretched but credulity unassailed. That all failed when a great skull-faced head of monstrous proportions, a Niño de la Tierra filling the tunnel whole, pushed through the smoke. This was beyond reason and that veneer of sanity was swept away. They broke.

The rout was madness. Those with shotguns began firing at the beast as it pulled itself forward. Yesil felt shot tear at his clothes and prick his arm. Beside him, he saw Arliss lurch forward, the back of his head blown in from a panicked shot poorly aimed. Yesil climbed and scrambled over those still defying with harmless thunder that thing before them. He pushed, shoved and ran, his trigger finger clicking over and again on empty chambers.

Yesil burst from the H-line, pushed and pushing amid his fleeing men. He had no idea what was happening behind him though the screams told a tale of horror. As the fleeing men stumbled over each other into the wider tunnel, they were met with a sight of utter nightmare. Two of the men who had fled before them were struggling on the ground, their bodies writhing with bugs. Their cries were muted, choked gargles as they suffered. One clawed against the wall opposite, trying to rise to his feet but unable. The other lay face down clawing at the dirt floor, a child of the earth five feet long clamping his leg in huge mandibles while it feasted. It was this sight that bottled the men coming into the wider tunnel. Those in the van had come to a halt but those in train only knew to fear what was behind. Yesil was borne under in a stumbling pile.

As Yesil struggled to rise beneath the knees and boots of others, he saw another great skull-faced giant race towards him. He was on his knees as the thing scuttled forward, its mandibles wide when an explosion roared from behind and the creature's head disintegrated in a noisome mess. As he stared at the twitching thing stopped a mere yard distant, a hand grabbed him under his right shoulder and pulled.

"¡Jefe! ¡Ven! ¡Ven!" It was Hector. "¡Prisa!"

Yesil rose and as he did, he saw three other large bugs in their midst. Two men had fled beyond the entrance and were running down the A-line as fast as they could. The rest were fighting; they had no choice. Picks were swinging wildly and another blast deafened the tunnel as Yesil grabbed up a fallen tool. Fear brings forth force never realized and Yesil joined in a brutal orgy of release.

"¡Detener! ¡Detener! Stop!" Hector was a foreman for a reason. His voice could carry, could command. "Jesse, give me that lantern!" Then to all with sober command, "We stay together! We separate, we die! ¿Lo tengo?"

Snapping his shotgun shut with a fresh shell loaded, Hector took the lantern and looked down the tunnel. Yesil turned as well and saw a shadow amongst the shadows lurching forward. Without further pause, Hector hurled the lantern down the H-line. As burning oil splashed on the tunnel walls, the monster was illuminated in its approach. As soon as the flames caught, masses began converging in purposeful immolation.

"¡Vamanose! ¡Juntos!"

Yesil was never one to overstep competence. One last look back showed him the two poor souls covered in bugs. They both still struggled feebly beneath their coverings. None had even uttered a suggestion to rescue them. That they had been beyond rescue since they first saw them was beyond doubt, but the thought passed through Yesil's mind that perhaps they should have tried or at least ended their sufferings. These were thoughts lost to pounding steps as he ran in the cover of others. The grunt that escaped his lips was all that he could summon for laughter and that was lost in the din of nightmare all about. That such a thought, mercy against horror, crossed his mind was the least credulous thing he'd encountered the whole day through.

They ran down the A-line, the slippery crunch of insects beneath their boots. As they ran, each tried swatting away those crawling on them as best they could while the swarming intrusion grew ahead of them. When a giant would come at them from an alcove or drift, they would gather around it and slaughter it en masse before resuming their flight, all under Hector's sharp commands. They passed one feasting on the head of a miner as the man still struggled in its grasp and tore it to pieces. They ran on leaving the man twitching in death, his head still in the maw of that monster. Yesil held his tongue, thoughts of how easy it would be to end that suffering he kept to himself.

When they came on another man gripped between two giants, they descended upon them with the same fury and tore the beasts apart. The man rescued was still alive, still very aware and screaming in Spanish for succor as smaller bugs scrambled over him.

"¡Vamanose! ¡Él está muerto!"

"But boss, he ain't dead."

"He will be. Do you want to die with him?"

"But…"

Yesil listened to this exchange and knew his course in an instant. Bold and decisive action was needed. Yesil buried his pick into the dying man's skull.

"Now he's dead. Let's go!" Yesil looked hard at the grim faces staring aghast at him in the thin light. "You heard him, let's go!"

At those words, the teaming bugs crawling over them all bit at once. Why they hadn't done so before, Yesil knew not but at that moment, it didn't matter. None were spared and of the seven men gathered there in that space, all spasmed in agony as assaults more painful than any bee-sting or ant-bite wracked their bodies. They swatted at themselves, clawing at their clothes and ripping them off to get at the offending vermin. And as these men jerked and twisted, that monstrous beast they had left behind burst from the darkness and began its slaughter. It crashed into the crowd, bowling them over and grasping one man in its mandibles. Chaos took over, the horror and panic amplified as this god of all things ugly and unholy latched itself onto the screaming man and scraped its labrum down his spine.

Horror beyond all bounds inspires desperate action and dulls the senses to all but the most incapacitating pain, and this eclipsed all nightmares Yesil had seen or dreamt. This was insanity of a most loathsome nature tearing its maxillae into the back of a man before their eyes as huge mandibles crushed and ground together, tearing the man to meat in their grasp. In spite of their pain, terror took hold. Half fled without regard of the others. Three men took their picks and buried them into the creature's head. Yesil, seeing the enormity of the beast, fled. In no terms could his mind come to grips with a potato bug twenty feet long from head to abdomen. His flight was automatic.

His flight was doomed. As he set in motion, the beast swept a long, pole-like leg, smashing the rout and throwing all nearby to ground. Without pause, Yesil scrambled back to his feet, pulling on another man, the lunk the Colonel had drawn on, to help him rise. In panic, the big man shoved Yesil aside in his own bid to escape. Thrown off balance, Yesil crashed against a decommissioned ore-cart and felt his head crack against iron.

Perspective altered in agonizing waves. Sound disappeared in a deafening crash. Vision rose from black to shadows of grim contrast flailing before him. He knew not where he was and his flesh pulsed in angry protest. He knew but pain and fear and that he must run, must get away. He tried to stand but failed. Grasping the cart behind him, he pulled himself to his feet and stood there swaying. When he turned to obey this primal need to flee, he was blocked by what he could not tell at first. Then as his eyes came at last to focus, his mind recalled the monstrosity now looming before him. With waste purging, he summoned words whispered in haste from his pious youth in acceptance of a fate he could no longer escape.

"Ey göklerde olan Babamız, İsmin mukaddes olsun; Melekûtun gelsin; Gökte olduğu..."

The thing before him moved slowly closer and closer and the closer it came, the more distinct the horror.

"...gibi yerde de senin iraden olsun; Gündelik ekmeğimizi bize bugün ver..."

Closer still and Yesil saw beneath that translucent armor that covered the head of the unholy beast. Beneath was a writhing mass as the individual parts of the whole became visible.

"...Ve bize borçlu olanlara bağışladığımız gibi, bizim borçlarımızı bize bağışla..."

The words came faster, sped by panic and a last-minute hope for succor or salvation for before him was confirmation of fears held dear, that here there truly was horror beyond rumor, damnation beyond understanding.

"...Ve bizi iğvaya götürme, fakat bizi şerirden kurtar..."

Beneath that smooth surface, millions of bugs swarmed, those nearest pressing their miniscule legs forth in anticipation from the smooth face of this god of damned things as Yesil leaned back over the ore-cart to delay the inevitable.

"...Çünkü melekût ve kudret ve izzet ebedlere kadar senindir."

The communal monster pressed itself to Yesil's face and the translucent bugs parted to accommodate. Waving legs, tiny and thick as hair, reached forth and took hold of his flesh, latching on and pulling. He pushed back with his arms but they plunged useless within that swarming mass. As the word "Amin" left his mouth, the pale, bloodless bugs forced their way into it. He gagged, he choked, he gnashed his teeth and pushed with his tongue, but still they forced their way in. He could feel them crunch, feel their legs kicking and clawing all throughout his mouth and, to his horror, writhing in his throat. There was no scream he could force, no reflex that would repulse those perversions. He gagged and choked as he felt himself slide further into that nightmare, pulled by a million grasping things. When he felt them start to gnaw on the edges of his soul, reason abandoned Yesil Batur.

He swam in a dream decrepit, rotten and noxious as this intrusion scoured his soul and feasted on the many sins therein. Cruel jaws tore free memories of prostitutes strangled in opium dreams or men similarly dispatched, of graves shallow dug and bribes paid to the furnace keeper beneath the smelter below the mill. Yesil Batur watched this decay torn free within him, sins lying like meat discarded on a butcher's floor, red sins and sins beyond redemption. And as the years of corruption were stripped from his soul, the detritus torn free and the damnations accumulated around the withered memory at their core, he laughed. He laughed unrestrained there within that nightmare for he recognized that singular stalk, that thread laid bare. He laughed for he saw the sins strewn about and cherished them more than the idealistic fraud found at the center. He laughed for he knew he was found worthy by that which he had mocked, that which he had disbelieved. He was found worthy for the price of souls harvested and the promise of more. Without pause, he joined those bugs gnawing and tearing at his last pretense of decency in a willing orgy of damnation.

With that, Yesil found himself crawling in pained ruin on the floor of the tunnel. Sickness overcame him and he vomited, heaving violently in the ultimate silence about. When the spasms subsided, he lay in his waste, staring at the twitching, kicking things his bile had brought forth. His head ached, pounding and throbbing in concert with the hundreds of bites his flesh had endured. His vision was blurred and uncertain, made exasperatingly worse as he wiped his face with an arm covered in ooze, a slime sprinkled throughout with bugs dead and dying. He saw them and he knew of the thousands still swarming about and he knew them now benign. Bodies too lay about, that one he'd picked himself in an act of decisive mercy and three others who failed their escapes and now were but flesh for vermin feasts.

He staggered delirious down that long hall through pools of flickering candlelight and the remains of his soul. As he placed one foot mindlessly before the other, he sorted through those sins scattered within. He raised in his arms each crime he had committed, raised their tattered remains to his lips and kissed them in cherished memory. He took them and placed them, one by one, in a cairn atop that withered remnant of forsaken virtue he had uprooted to secure his doom, to spare his life. Twenty-three years his soul had rotted upon this creek, in this town named for a dead man's warning. For twenty-three years, he had reigned a Sultan untouchable, power and cruel, decadent pleasure forming him as he formed now this tribute to his sins where the last of his scruples had clung.

Yesil Batur was no fool. He held no illusion his passage came without cost. He could feel the insects crawling within him, deeper than his stomach could contend. He could feel their dying spasms within his intestines and he could smell their odor still in his soul. He felt the eggs they seeded within the deepest reaches of his psyche. This thing from whence they came, this unholy Child of the Earth, held no mercy for Yesil had seen within that horror the truth it deigned to share. It was far more unforgiving than the Colonel ever prophesied, a truth he would have to share with his old friend.

His steps were slow and tortured. His stomach cramped and rebelled but had no strength remaining to expel what moved within. His body ached from the thousand wounds suffered. His mind was dull and numb, his thoughts focused upon his revelation, his oath of fealty forced. In the belly of that mountain which granted his fortune, Yesil Batur sloughed the last remnants of human virtue from his heart, enslaved to the desires that clung to the cruel thing that remained. And as he walked, as he staggered uncertainly toward that far distant adit, his delusions turned to details of deeds yet done, of murders intimately planned. Decadence so anticipated filled his mouth and the soft crunch of mindless mastication echoed with his steps through the silence of the tunnel.

THE LION, THE WITCH, AND THE WALRUS
J.T. Haven

Jimmy Ransom, Jr. couldn't remember the when or the who concerning how he'd acquired the nickname "The Walrus." But he knew the why. And, to be clear, it had nothing to do with his love of the Beatles' hit song "I Am the Walrus." Rather, the nickname came to light because of Jimmy's oversized, damned-near tusk-like front teeth, his stocky stature, and the fact that he'd worn his hair shaved close to his round knob of a head his whole life. Sadly, having a heart of gold seems to get you nowhere if you resemble a creature that was clearly the butt of a joke shared by Mother Nature and God during the stand-up comedy routine called Creation. For as long as Jimmy could remember, he had been the Walrus. That was the way it was and there was nothing this now forty-something seemingly eternal bachelor could do about it.

Having finished a long, hot day in the bucket seat of his excavator, Jimmy climbed down from "Bessie," wiped his forehead with his trusty blue bandana, and took off into the nearby woods to relieve his aching bladder. To Jimmy, one of the perks of being a solo contractor on a small bid job for the county was not having the hassle of Port-O-Lets and other big site, big crew formalities. Gotta go? You just wander off into the trees and let 'er rip.

Fly down, wang out, and pee dribbling its second finale encore, Jimmy thought he saw a flash of red in his periphery. Turning his head to the right, he almost yanked his pecker clean off when the red-headed woman standing inches from him said, "Nice pistol you got there, handsome."

"What? Oh gawd, I think I pissed on your dress, lady. Where did you—"

"Where I came from isn't important."

Struggling to repackage his package, Jimmy blinked a few times in disbelief as the sun cut through the pine trees, creating a glow around the woman's head. A radiant glow that looked like fire, a lot like fire. "Ma'am, I hate to tell you this, but I think your hair is on fire."

Reaching a hand up casually to pat out the flames, the strange woman said, "Ah, so it is. Damn sun can't keep his flames to himself. That's what I get for burning a star. Love 'em and leave 'em evidently isn't a philosophy he embraces."

"Um, I'm sorry. Who did you say you were?"

"I didn't. Because it's not important."

With this proclamation, the woman turned on her heels. Assuming she had heels or feet or even legs. The way she glided along the pine needle and leaf carpeting, and due to the floor-length length of her scarlet dress, Jimmy could only assume she had heels.

Within seconds, Jimmy's decision was clearly made for him when the woman said, "I have beer chilling in the fridge."

Decision made. Jimmy followed her deep into the forest, without further question.

Eyes closed, Jimmy Ransom Jr. heard strange noises and smelled peculiar smells. He questioned whether he might be in a zoo. Maybe the lady in the forest ran a petting zoo or an exotics ranch. Quite a few of those places had popped up in the area lately. Great for locals and tourists alike. Also, they were a perfect place to take a date, or so the billboards claimed. Jimmy wouldn't know, he'd never been to one—on a date or otherwise. In fact, he'd never even been on a date, so he really had no clue.

Carefully, as if testing the waters of a pond with a toe before midnight skinny dipping, he pried one sweet tea-colored eye open. Holy shit! He was hanging, maybe thirty feet up, looking down onto an open sand pit encircled by metal cages. In the cages were animals of all sorts, from bears to boa constrictors to lions. Goddamn lions!

Glancing down his horizontal body, Jimmy saw the rigging and canvas that held him aloft; it looked like the kind of setup a hang glider might use—not that Jimmy had ever been hang gliding, but he'd seen them on TV at least once. A cocoon of black, shiny fabric supported him from just under his armpits down to his ankles. Arms tucked in by his sides, he realized his hands were tingling as if they were asleep.

"Ah, you're awake. Welcome back, handsome." Standing between a caged white tiger and an imprisoned gorilla that looked like a pissed off cousin of King Kong, was the woman from the woods.

"Where am I?" is what Jimmy wanted to ask, however, his mouth appeared to have been sealed shut. Running his tongue along the inside of his lips, the captive blue-collar fellow felt twine running vertically inside his mouth. Holy shit take two! The bitch in red had sewn his mouth shut. Daddy had always warned him about gingers.

"Oh, don't be upset about the handiwork I did on your mouth. Might be a bit sore when the numbing agent and pain meds wear off but, more than likely, you won't live that long. So, it won't matter."

Jimmy's head pounded and his heart raced. Between beats and pounds, he tried to remember anything and everything that had happened after he'd followed her home. He recalled that he'd not seen a driveway in front of the crumbling Victorian mansion, only a slightly overgrown walking path. No power or phone lines that he could see, but so much of that was run underground these days that he wasn't too surprised by this. No mailbox or even slot on the door, but maybe she had a post office box in the nearby town of Coldspring. All in all, it was an odd sight in the middle of the National Forest but not odd enough to send him fleeing for his life.

He remembered entering the house via a creaky front door and following the woman into an old-timey parlor or sitting room of sorts— lots of maroon velvet and lace aged yellow. The red-headed stranger encouraged him to have a seat in a high-backed, leather chair. Following this, she had said she wanted to slip into something more comfortable then would snag him a beer. While waiting for her to return, Jimmy thought he might have dozed off briefly, but he wasn't sure. When she finally came back into the room, though, he snapped awake. Wide awake.

Her red, floor-length gown had been replaced by a red and black zebra-striped bra and panties set—the kind only "those type of women" wore. There were two-inch-long zippers across each nipple region and a longer, wider zipper guarding her hidden lady treasures.

"Like what you see, big boy?" the mysterious woman had asked. All he'd been able to do in response was clear his throat and nod in wide-eyed appreciation.

Physically back in the present, Jimmy mentally replayed the memory of their sexual rendezvous, including the odd-tasting beer he'd lapped from her bellybutton, lower back, and about half-a-dozen other more unmentionable places. He would have continued the pleasurable playback; however, the fabric that suspended him from the ceiling was starting to tent southward embarrassingly and painfully. Besides, Jimmy couldn't seem to remember anything after he'd reached the "O moment". Everything in his memory, after that, faded to a fuzzy black.

"Oh, lover boy, you about ready to come down and play? Are you feeling sufficiently rested and ready to run?" Lady Sexy Von Crazy called up to him as she sauntered over to a red button affixed to one of the gray cement blocks that made up the walls.

As she depressed the button, two things happened simultaneously: the rig Jimmy was cocooned in sank toward the floor and the animals all fell into silence. Eerie, complete silence. Starting to officially panic, Jimmy jerked his head around looking for any hope of escape. Nothing. He couldn't see any plausible way out of his current predicament.

Stopping the winch—or whatever mechanism she was using to raise and lower the rig—about three feet from the floor, she smiled and winked at her captive. "We're going to have so much fun. Just you, me, and—hmm, who will it be this time?"

Walking around the assorted cages, the woman addressed the inhabitants in turn. "Maybe Jacob the Anaconda? He's a slippery one with a foul squeeze. Or how about Travis the Panther. Sleek and sexy with a nasty, toothy attitude. No, I know who hasn't been out to play in a while. How about you, Marcus?"

With utter terror, Jimmy allowed his eyes to meander from the woman's face down to the cage she stood beside. Beyond the shiny, silver bars crouched—as if ready to pounce—the biggest lion Jimmy had ever seen. The tawny beast's eyes were the size of baseballs and his canine teeth were—believe it or not—significantly larger than Jimmy's own front teeth.

"Yes, the lion, the witch, and the walrus. What a story this will be to share with my devotees!"

The thought of people following or worshipping this bat-shit crazy lady was beyond thinkable for small town, southern boy Jimmy Ransom, Jr. But wait, hadn't he willingly followed her into the forest? And, prior to his waking a half-hour or so ago, hadn't he worshipped at her feet as she spanked him with a yellow, plastic fly swatter and called him names that would make sailors blush? Shame and regret coursed through his veins, straight to his weary heart.

"Give me a few minutes to slip into something more appropriate. Would you like another beer? Silly me. I forgot that I'd laced your lips shut. Oh, well. I guess there'll be no last supper or final bit of frothy hops for you, my handsome boy. Sorry. Be right back."

Once she'd vanished down a side hall, Jimmy did his best fish in a net impersonation—flipping and flopping as best he could, regrettably realizing that she'd bound his ankles together and his arms still seemed to be asleep or in a drugged state. He might as well have been a mute paraplegic. All he could do was wait in abject terror for her to return. Which came sooner than he would have liked.

Sauntering back in, the witchy woman—previously wearing the red dress, then trussed up in the black and red zebra bra and panties, then back to the red dress—now donned a pair of skin-tight, black capris; knee-high riding boots; a clingy red, spaghetti-strap tank top; and a safari hat. Jimmy took a moment to rack his brain, searching for the term for that unmistakable style of hat. One like the historical explorers wore. A kind of hardhat for the jungle bound. What were they called? Pitch hats? Pint helmets? If there'd been an audience viewing this scene, they would have been yelling the name at the screen and throwing popcorn at his dimwittedness. But try as he might, Jimmy couldn't recall the name. Sorry, viewers. Maybe later.

"Here I am! I'm back!" the woman announced as she did a ta-da type of gesture that made Jimmy roll his eyes and exhale in exasperation.

"Let me get Marcus into his starting position then I'll come back for you, Mr. Walrus."

Jimmy watched as the woman pulled a small remote control from her cleavage and pushed one of the buttons. The lion's cage began to roll along a track toward the wall to the right side of the room. Along the wall were five metal, roll-down doors like those used for individual car garage bays. As the cage approached, the middle door rolled up and the cage passed through. Glaring light prevented Jimmy from seeing what was beyond the door.

"Bye, bye, beastly baby. Mama will see you soon." She raised a hand and wiggled her scarlet-painted fingertips toward the exiting cage and its inhabitant as the two disappeared behind the lowering metal door. Then she turned to face her prisoner. "Now to prep you for the festivities."

Walking over to the wall-mounted control she'd pressed earlier, the Witch—as she'll be referred to from now on—whacked the button and Jimmy slammed to the ground, silky cocoon and all. What looked like soft sand, turned out to be tightly packed sand. Jimmy grunted on impact.

"Oh, did I hurt my little walrus of a lamb? Me so sorry."

Baby talk did not do anything for Jimmy in this precarious moment. In fact, if anything, it enraged him further. As did the realization that he still couldn't move the upper half of his body. At all. No action of shoulders, arms, or upper torso. He could rotate his head and he could move his legs to the extent that the ankle bindings allowed, but that was it.

"Oh, stop fidgeting. You'll be free soon enough." As she spoke—keeping a safe distance from Jimmy's flailing legs—the Witch untethered the silk cocoon, letting it fall to the ground around his body. Then she deftly clipped a carabiner and chain to the back of the black, nylon harness Jimmy now noticed he was wearing. With the push of another button on her handy-dandy remote control, the Witch's prey was dragged across the clearing toward one of the garage bay doors—luckily, Jimmy thought, not the same one the lion had exited through.

The chain ran between the smooth concrete floor of that end of the room and a notch in the lower lip of the door. Moving at a rapid clip, Jimmy felt certain that he was about to smash headfirst into the metal barrier. However, as he braced for the impact, the door began to roll up. Instead of slamming into it, Jimmy found himself flying off a cliff and falling into a deep quarry or man-made, four-sided canyon of some sort. Maybe meeting the door up close and personal would have been preferable, Jimmy wondered.

As gravity took over, the chain's role seemed to become one of stopping Jimmy's forward momentum. With a snapping jerk, the chain came to an abrupt halt fifteen feet or so from the rocky bottom of the cavern; at which time, Jimmy promptly peed his pants. The dangling dude was uncertain whether this had occurred due to the relief of not hitting the snaggle-toothed rock bedding below or due to the sheer need to relieve himself. What he did know for certain was that he was in a heap of trouble. Just below him sat Marcus, and the gargantuan lion had proceeded to start licking his chops as if Jimmy resembled a T-bone steak wrapped in lamb chops and slathered in copious amounts of bacon grease.

"Have no fear, boys, the lady of the hour has arrived."

Jimmy rolled his eyes again as the Witch floated down toward them, dangling ever so gracefully from red parachute. Upon landing, the prisoner hoped that the lion would pounce on the Witch and tear her to shreds. But, of course, the beast didn't. Instead, the damn thing began to purr like an obnoxiously oversized, death-machine kitten.

"Hello, Marcus-Warcus." After unclipping herself from the parachute, the Witch patted the lion's head and made kissy noises at it. "Are you hungry? Doesn't walrus sound like a tasty treat? Jimmy, what do you think?"

Racking his brain, Jimmy couldn't remember ever telling the Bitch—oops, the Witch—his name. However, if that were the oddest part of this whole f-ed up situation, Jimmy was willing to let that tiny storyline hiccup go. How she controlled the deadly beast, now giving her kisses like a damned golden retriever, was more of a mystery. This woman really might be an honest-to-Satan witch, Jimmy decided. He had no idea how to defeat a witch and only slightly less knowledge about how to best a lion in combat or chase. If his arms had been functional—wait, fingers wiggled, wrists trembled, elbows bent. Jimmy could use his arms and, in celebration, quickly did the sign of the cross with his left arm and in reverse order, but it seemed like the right thing to do in the given moment.

"Oh honey, that sort of spell don't work on me and sweet baby Jesus can't save you from Marcus. He wasn't a lion tamer. I don't think. Sorry." The Witch wiped her lion-spittle covered face with a black lace handkerchief she'd pulled from her cleavage—of course—then whispered something in the lion's ear. Immediately, the lion trotted off into the distance and the Witch said, "Now that feeling has returned to your arms, this will be more of a fair fight. Marcus hates when his prey is too easy to catch."

Pulling a giant knife out—not from her cleavage this time, but from a sheath on her thigh; although Jimmy thought that would have been rather amusing to see—the Witch cut the zip ties that had been pinning her captive's leg together. Noticing the dampness of his Levi's, she shook her head. "Men just can't hold their liquor or their bladders. What is wrong with your gender?"

Feeling a bit light-headed, possibly due to the recent restoration in the blood flow of his circulatory system or the wearing off of whatever drugs or spell she'd used on him, Jimmy began to mumble a response to her query. However, he gave up after a few minutes and supposed he might have been rambling in order to stall whatever violence was inevitably coming. As if reading his mind, the Witch began to explain what would be occurring.

"Marcus has gone to the far side of the arena to give you a fair start. After I've climbed up the cliff to my viewing box, I'll remotely release your harness latch. Marcus won't begin the hunt until I sound the signal. You up for this, big boy?"

What?!?! Who in their right mind would be up for whatever this insanity was?

Before Jimmy could wrap his brain further around this whacked out situation or figure out a strategy for avoiding being Marcus' lunch, the Witch disappeared somewhere behind him. With a click, Jimmy felt the harness give way and he fell onto the rocks below. Adrenaline masked the pain of his scraped shin, bloodied knees, and raw, bleeding palms. As a loud horn sounded, Jimmy jumped up, more like a jackrabbit than a walrus.

With no idea which way to run or where to hide, Jimmy started running as hard as he could in any and every direction that seemed easiest and fastest. In the distance, he heard the Witch call out, "Run, Walrus, run!"

Oh, no. Did she really just make a *Forrest Gump* joke at his expense? If he ever had the chance—

His thoughts and body froze as he heard a growling roar, way too close for comfort. What the hell was an out-of-shape, highway road crew guy going to do against a goddamn, enchanted King of the Jungle? Jimmy had no idea, but he'd have to think of something. And quick.

Within what felt like few precious minutes, the arena's human prey realized that he'd backed himself into a corner—well, fronted himself into a wall actually, but there was a minimal amount of lucidity running his ship at that moment. A sheer, rock cliff stood in front of him. To his right, was a path overgrown with spiked and thorny vegetation. To the left, dense trees and undergrowth—way too thick for him to get through. And behind him was Marcus. Jimmy knew this because he could hear the lion's low growl and practically smell the beast's rancid breath.

At this pivotal moment in the Walrus' life, he knew he had nothing to lose. This inkling allowed Jimmy to access parts of himself he'd never known were there before. Magical parts that were deep inside and well above the area he had previously considered his magic zone.

Frothing through the loosening stitches that caged his mouth and with a gleam in his eye that Jimmy had never known before, he grabbed a thick branch and began to swing it wildly at the lion's huge head. Like a lion tamer from legends of old, Jimmy's manic display affected the lion in an odd and peculiar way. Despite the branch never making physical contact with mane or muzzle, Marcus froze in his pursuit and began to back away from Jimmy.

In the distance, someone laid on the horn like a trucker trying to get around a granny in the fast-pass lane. The Witch seemed to be signaling her vicious pet to stop messing around and go in for the kill. However, her placid pet wasn't listening to her anymore. A new master was in this f-ed up town, and his name was Jimmy the Walrus.

With chest puffed up and chin held high, Jimmy ripped a vine off a nearby tree. Thick branch in one hand and verdant whip in the other, the unexpected lion tamer fought back his attacker—chasing him all the way back to the place where they'd started this sick game. In a seemingly panicked state, the Witch descended from her high-rise throne and met Marcus and Jimmy under the dangling harness. "What? This isn't possible. What is happening here?"

Using his stronger-than-average tongue to work his threaded lips free, the Walrus stretched the aching flesh of his face then replied, "Bitch, your pussy just got walrus-whipped."

The Witch burst out in laughter. Not a giggle or a tee-hee-hee. But gut-busting, tears-gushing, guffawing laughter. Stunned, Jimmy wasn't sure what to do or say, so he simply stood in his warrior's pose with leafy whip and bark-bound weapon in hand. Once she'd regained her breath and composure, the Witch turned to her fanged companion and said, "Okay, boy. He's all yours."

As blood flew and fangs ripped flesh, Jimmy's last thoughts were about what an amazing one-liner that would have been for the hero of an action movie and how glad he was that those were the last words he would ever utter. Now, if only the bitch had recorded them, he would be the next viral, internet sensation—even if it would be posthumously. Oh, and—he didn't forget—two words popped into his head at Jimmy's moment of death: pith helmet. He had remembered, before it was too late. Thank goodness—that changed everything.

GRIME
Hannah Shannon

"I don't know about this place," I said as I crushed a bug under my heel.

Artemis shot me an impatient look as she flipped her thick blonde hair over her shoulder. She gently set down the bucket of hot, soapy water she'd carried in from the dilapidated kitchen.

"It's not like we can afford anything better," she snapped.

I looked around doubtfully at the dingy yellow walls and threadbare carpet, thinking for the millionth time that there had to be something better somewhere. But I knew she was right. We'd spent months scouring the city for anything that would fit our budget, and this was it. This shack in the middle of nowhere, coated in tobacco grime and speckled with bug refuse. I sighed, defeated, and Artemis softened.

"Baby, baby," she cooed, stepping across the tiny living room to wrap her arms around me. "It's going to be fine, I promise. We'll scrub the walls and rip out the carpet, bug bomb the hell out of it, and seal the cracks. By the time we're done you won't even believe what a dump it used to be." Her blue eyes shone with something like hope, and I caved.

"Alright," I said as I returned her embrace. "I trust you."

"Good." She rose to her tiptoes and kissed me briefly; the kind of kiss that says *shut up and get to work*.

So I did, and so did she. Armed with five-gallon buckets of steamy fragrance and a whole lot of sponges, we each claimed a wall and got to work. The runoff stank like death, and I was gagging before I'd even cleaned three feet of the wall. Cleaned…that was a generous assessment. Each layer I scraped off only revealed more nastiness. Fly spots upon fly spots, smoke grime upon older smoke grime, and some kind of strange brown haze which smelled like rotting meat.

"God, it's like someone got atomized in here." I stepped away to catch my breath, but it was no use. The whole room smelled like floral-scented rot. Artemis looked a little green herself.

"It's pretty bad," she admitted. "Maybe we should just paint over it. It would take less time."

"Yeah, but then we'd know what was behind the paint."

"Fair."

We went back to it in silence, splattering our arms and torsos with disgusting runoff no matter how hard we tried not to. Artemis took a few breaks to smoke, first outside, but then inside because it didn't seem to matter anyway. By the time we'd finished two walls, the sun was starting to go down. I flipped on the light to see what we'd accomplished. It was decidedly underwhelming.

"Do you think the paint is just yellow?" I asked doubtfully.

"No," she said with a sigh. "I managed to find a bit of white over here, but it's just so dirty. My arms hurt. I don't want to do anymore today."

I didn't want to sleep in the house with it in that condition, but there was no way around it. I didn't want to admit it, but my shoulders were aching too. The walls we'd cleaned were certainly brighter than the ones we hadn't, but there wasn't nearly enough of a difference to make six hours of hard labor feel worthwhile.

"I'll buy paint tomorrow," I said. "Screw this."

She granted me a tired, flat smile which was just this side of I-told-you-so. We slept in a mosquito tent in sleeping bags on the floor that night; our furniture would stay in storage until we had this place completely debugged. I wasn't about to let my grandma's antique dresser get contaminated.

Artemis was working the next day, so I took it upon myself to buy paint with money we didn't really have. I didn't bother to cover the carpet. It was ruined anyway, and we were planning to tear it up, so what was the point? The work went a lot faster, and was infinitely more satisfying. By the time I had to go pick her up from work, each of the four walls plus the ceiling were coated in bright white paint. The room seemed bigger somehow, as if just eliminating the nastiness gave me room to breathe.

I showed up at her work exhausted, covered in paint splatter and smiling.

"Oh! Hard at work today?" She was so beautiful when she beamed at me like that.

"You know it, darlin'! I can't wait for you to see, it looks like a whole new room."

"Did you give it any color?"

"Not today, I just wanted to get the white down. We can do an accent wall on payday if you want to."

"Yes!" She clapped her hands and bounced in her seat excitedly. "We'll do a teal wall in the front room and a rose-colored wall in our bedroom."

"Teal? Really?"

"What, is blue better? Maybe it would be. I guess it depends on what color you painted the rest of the room."

"Um…white."

"Yes," she said impatiently, "But what kind of white?"

I blinked at her. "The kind…that is white?"

She stared at me flatly for a second, then rolled her eyes. "I guess I'll just find out when we get there."

"It's white! What's there to find out?"

"The tone," she said impatiently. "Is it true white? Eggshell? Ivory? There are so many different kinds, and if you have a white with a red tone and your accent wall is red, it makes the room look a little darker than if you have a blue accent wall. It's subtle, but I promise I'm not making it up."

"White is white," I said stubbornly. "But you tell me what color to get and I'll get it."

"That's all I ask." Her impatience melted away into a beaming smile as we turned onto our street. "Oh, I can't wait to see!"

She really couldn't, apparently. As soon as I'd parked she was out of the car, running up the cracked, weedy path to burst through the flimsy door. I followed at a more leisurely pace, giving her a chance to decide what kind of white I'd chosen. Leave it to me to choose the wrong white. Trust her to tell me if I did.

"Is this some kind of joke?" She stormed back out of the house before I'd even made it to the front door. Her blue eyes flashed dangerously, and her plump lips curled back into a thin snarl.

"Wrong one?" I asked sheepishly.

"Wrong what? Wrong dingy nastiness?" She spun on her heel and stalked back into the house, shaking her head. "You're a piece of work, you know that? Getting me all excited just to bring me back to this! What did you expect, road head?"

"What are you talking about?" But as I followed her into the house, I saw. Apart from the white paint which had seeped into the carpet, the room looked the same as it had that morning before I'd started, as if the grime had swallowed up my work. Even the ceiling looked the same.

"I can't imagine what else you were expecting," she snapped. "You knew I'd see it. You knew I'd be pissed. Why even get paint on the carpet? On yourself? What the hell is your problem?"

"Artie." I finally found my voice. "Honey, calm down. I did paint it, I swear."

"What did you do, water it down first?!"

"No, swear to God. There are three new coats of paint on these walls. Or...there were when I left."

She opened her mouth to speak, but stopped and put up her hands. She took a few deep breaths, then glared at me. "I'm going to bed. If you want to join me...ever again...you'll fix this." With that, she marched into the bedroom and slammed the door behind her.

A moment later, I heard her scream. "Artie!" I rushed to the door, but she'd locked it. "Artie, are you okay?"

"Go away!"

Ah. A tantrum. Fine, whatever. Sighing, I rolled my aching shoulders and went to get the paint. I'd bought enough to cover the whole house, but that was fine. If going into debt on paint was going to make her happy, I would do it. I couldn't see that it would do much good; the house's grime seemed insatiable. But whatever. Back to it.

Sweat began rolling down my shoulders as I took to the walls again. I didn't feel that warm, but anger did weird things to my body chemistry, so I ignored the incessant drip-drip on my shoulders. I worked in silence for an hour before I realized that something was different. The light in the room had changed, as if a thick cloud was rolling over the sun. Only there was no sun. Confused, I looked up at the overhead light.

My jaw dropped open and I snapped it shut. Above me, pouring out of the light fixture, were millions of roaches. Big ones, little ones, in every shade of disgusting brown and yellow, they crawled over the fixture and down the walls. Some lost their footing and dropped, bouncing off of the carpet. My stomach heaved. I wanted to run, but they covered the doors. I watched as the pristine wall I had just painted turned dingy and gross before my very eyes.

"Artie!"

They were falling all over me: on my head, my arms, my shoulders, crawling down my back into my pants, skittering over my shoes. I flicked them off, but more came. My shirt was full of them, and I ripped it off.

"Artie, wake up! Shit!"

As I spoke, one crawled in my mouth. I crushed it between my teeth, slapping at my face, crushing at least five more who were trying to get into my nose and ears. I lunged at the bedroom door, breaking it apart and squishing a hundred more bugs with my shoulder. The bedroom wasn't nearly as bad as the living room, but the little shits were infiltrating, skirting the walls. The tent in the center of the room was jumping.

"Artie, come out of there, we have to go!"

She didn't answer, but I knew she was awake. She had to be.

"Damn it, Artemis, this is not the time to be a brat!" In my adrenaline-fueled panic, I ripped the net in half. She stared up at me, wide-eyed and silent, twitching and jerking on the floor.

"Get up; we have to get out of here!"

She didn't answer. Something was wrong. One of her eyes slid away, looking at the wall, while the other was locked on me. She opened her mouth, and a guttural sound croaked out. I stood over her, shaking.

"Please get up," I whispered.

Her funky eye started to drip. Tears, then something milky. Her tongue wagged like she was trying to speak. As I watched, her eye exploded in a red mist, her tongue burst open, and roaches poured to the floor. They surged out of her, nose, ears, eyes, mouth, covering her body, stripping her skin as they went. Pools of blood disappeared as quickly as they formed, absorbed by the seething mass.

My first instinct was to hurtle head-first out of the window, but it was caked in layer upon layer of the clicking, ravenous insects. They fell like

126

rain off of the doorframe. I ducked my head and bolted through. They were up to my knees before I reached the living room. No matter how I swatted and kicked, they swarmed over my body.

Fire. Kill it with fire.

I fumbled for my lighter as I stumbled toward the door. My foot collided with something hard, sending bugs scattering as it clattered to the floor. *The paint sprayer. Aerosol.* A primal scream tore from my throat as I lifted it out of the writhing mass, pulled the trigger, and flicked the lighter. The fireball cleared my path. Flaming bugs ran inches before they fell, lighting their fellow pests. The fresh paint and tired, dry carpet fed the flames eagerly.

The roaches were all over the front door. I blasted it, reaching through the flame to turn the blazing hot handle. One final blast behind me for good measure and I tossed the can inside. I heard it explode as I rolled over the dry, lumpy lawn, squishing bugs and putting out the flames which licked my body.

They were still in my hair, my clothes. I shook out the first and stripped out of the second, running for my life to the car. The burns on my hands and legs didn't even register as I turned the key in the ignition. It wasn't until my blistered palm sloughed off on the steering wheel that I even noticed. Screaming, I flicked the dead skin onto the floor. It was instantly seized by a handful of stowaways. I was blind with pain and terror. I didn't see the turn. I was airborne before I could hope to correct it, plummeting down into the black quarry water.

The next few days are a blur. The fire had caught the attention of the locals, and there were witnesses to my accident. They tell me I swam to the surface on my own, but I distinctly remember a pair of strong arms ripping me through the driver's side window. Maybe it was an unsung hero. Maybe it was Artemis' ghost, I don't know. After what I saw, I wasn't about to discount the supernatural.

The official story is that she died in a fire. Everybody knew she smoked like a chimney. Everybody knew that we'd been painting, and that the house was a deathtrap. Of course it was just a terrible accident. The fire marshal was very sorry for my loss, and the insurance company paid out without too much dithering.

It didn't take long to get rid of the property. I sold the land to a man who had big plans for a luxury spa and high-class hobby ranch. For all he was concerned, the fire simply saved him a step in the process. I was just happy to get away from the constant reminder.

"So this was the foundation?" he asked as we stood on the spot where she died.

"Yeah."

"Mm. Crumbling. Easy enough to get rid of. What the--!" He slapped his arm, leaving a brown streak.

"Roaches," he said with a grimace. "I hate roaches."

TARANTULA HAWK
Kevin Folliard

A high buzz startled Brock Morgan awake. His temples pounded. Sickness quivered over his skin. The bedroom blurred into focus.

"Good morning," came a honeysuckle voice.

The petite, raven-haired beauty he had wooed last night swarmed his memory. She had agreed to join him for a nightcap at his San Antonio ranch. He remembered escorting her through the door. Struggling to open a bottle of wine. Then . . .

The rest of the evening remained hazy. He faced the other side of the bed.

Empty.

His right wrist snagged. Metal clinked. Handcuffs chained his arm to a rung of the oak backboard. He tugged, but the cuffs held. "Shit!"

"Pay attention, Morgan," came the woman's voice.

Morgan glanced around the room.

"The nightstand."

A tablet was propped upon the left side table. The screen showed the woman, long fingers folded, small nose and expressive eyes rimmed by half-moon spectacles. Her dark hair twisted into a tight bun.

"You didn't even recognize me." Her thin lips smiled. "This was so easy that I'm almost disappointed."

"Listen, I might have agreed to some kinky thing last night, but—"

"Shut up. My name is Deborah Chen. I'm a research scientist and toxicologist."

Morgan's stomach sank. "Dr. Chen. I do remember you." He lowered his right arm. The chain of the handcuffs slackened. "I'm sorry you lost your job. There are many unfortunate drawbacks—"

129

"Please!" the woman hissed. "Don't act like downsizing was some unavoidable necessity, Morgan. My team was on the verge of curing a serious degenerative nerve disease. But you'd rather make billions pedaling slow, ineffective treatments. You make money off sick people, not cured people."

Morgan tugged the handcuffs again. He took a calming breath and scoured the room for his phone. Nobody would find him here. Not for days.

"I understand you're angry," Morgan said. "I'm sure we can reach an understanding. Tell me where the keys are, maybe we can forget this entire encounter."

"The keys are at the foot of the bed," she said.

Inches from Morgan's toes, two small keys gleamed on a silver ring. He shuffled down a few inches before the handcuffs snagged. He stretched his foot. Wiggled his toe. He could almost reach them.

Suddenly something fluttered from the ceiling. A humongous dark blue insect with a metallic sheen and rust-colored wings glided down. Its spidery legs sprawled atop the keys.

Morgan's foot recoiled.

The bug was several inches long—the size of a human finger. Its clawed front legs hooked into the sheets. Its long abdomen ended into a sharp point. Huge, black eyes bulged and antennae curled from its brow like calligraphy.

"That, Morgan, is a tarantula hawk," Dr. Chen explained. "The largest wasp on Earth. They deliver one of the most painful stings of any insect, second only to the bullet ant."

Morgan's stomach quivered.

"I soaked the keys in a solution that mimics this wasp's favorite nectar. Tarantula hawks are not fatally venomous to humans," she explained. "So before I left, I injected you with something that *is*. Potent venom of my own devising."

"Jesus!" Morgan yanked the handcuffs again.

The wasp shook orange wings. Its stinger flexed.

"By my estimate you have twenty minutes," Chen said, "maybe thirty, to counteract this poison before your heart gives up."

Morgan fell still. His chest pounded. Skull throbbed. The creeping sensation tripled over his skin, and he realized he wasn't hungover after all. "You've killed me." Tears spilled down his cheeks.

The tarantula hawk's mandibles twitched over the shimmering keys as it lapped at synthetic nectar.

He wrenched his arm again. Screamed for help.

"Panicking will make the venom act faster," Dr. Chen said in a controlled, icy tone.

"What's the use?" Morgan choked. "Even if I called an ambulance right now, they'd never make it out here in time."

"Then pay attention." Her spectacles gleamed over that calculating smile. "There are *two* keys on the ring, Morgan. Across the room, in a locked box, is the anti-venom."

Morgan spotted a metal mesh case, sitting on the dresser across the room. A chrome padlock secured the lid.

"Use one key to remove the cuffs, the other to open the box," Chen explained. "Inject the antivenom *directly* into your heart and you will live. But I'm warning you . . ."

The tarantula hawk gnashed its spiny front legs.

"One sting from your little guest will cause debilitating agony." Her smile widened. "Act fast. But act carefully."

"Shit." Morgan cautiously stretched his toe. He tried to maneuver it under the key ring, but the insect's stinger hovered less than an inch from that spot. "You would kill over this?" he asked. "Getting fired? You're smart, Dr. Chen. You couldn't find another job?"

"Look at the screen, Morgan."

He glanced back. The tablet showed a lovely dark-haired little girl, with a silver butterfly hairpin, a red floral print dress, and deep brown eyes.

"My daughter Lily died in the year since you terminated our life-saving research." Her high voice dripped malice. "Countless others died as well."

Morgan gasped. "I didn't kill your daughter." He attempted to nudge the tarantula hawk's wing, to encourage it to fly away.

"You certainly did not save her."

As soon as his toe touched the insect, its bronze wings vibrated. It ascended then landed on Morgan's right foot. Prickly legs stabbed his ankle as it crawled up his leg. He froze.

"You're a prowling spider, Morgan, preying upon the world's most vulnerable."

"Morgan Pharmaceuticals helps sick people! You're mixed up!" He shifted his right leg toward the edge of the bed, carrying the hawk away from the keys.

"You take advantage."

Morgan slid his left foot as close as he could to the key ring. He stretched, grunted, and managed to get his big toe on the tip of one small key. The keys were creeping toward the edge of the bed, if they fell over, that was it.

He used his heel to apply pressure to the mattress and sink the keys closer, all the while balancing the wasp on his right leg as still as possible.

The manacle dug into his wrist. Sensation faded from his chained arm. Fingers tingled. That quivering sensation was spreading to his head.

His right leg started trembling. The tarantula hawk took to the air again, a blue-bronze blur. It landed—back on the keys. Morgan kept his toe still, half under the key ring.

Sweat ran down his face.

He struggled for a breath.

"I know this won't bring my daughter back," Chen said. "But I take small pleasure in watching you struggle. Do you know why they're called tarantula hawks?"

"They . . . fight them?" He panted. "Eat them?"

"They're nectivorous mostly. But when the time is right, the females hunt, sting, and paralyze a tarantula. They drag the hapless spider to a burrow and lay eggs in them. The wasp larvae eat their way out of the still-living spider's husk. How utterly fascinating that such a fierce creature could become so powerless."

"I'm not a fucking tarantula!" Morgan yanked his arm as far as it would go. He strained his leg and worked his toe through the key ring. The wasp stirred, then calmed.

"A tarantula doesn't think of itself as a monster, Morgan," Chen said. "I'm sure you don't either."

Morgan's head swam as he turned toward the tablet. Dr. Chen's wide eyes, round head, and shiny black dome of hair had taken a cruel, insectoid quality.

"Nature has a peculiar way of ensuring that even monsters have monsters. I never thought I could become this. My daughter would not be proud. But then again, I've given you a sporting chance, haven't I?"

The room spun. Morgan focused on the bulbous creature curled over his toe. The keys continued to glisten with the synthetic nectar. It was now or never.

Morgan yanked his toe upward. The tarantula hawk sailed into the air. The keys flipped, arched, and plopped on Morgan's stomach. The hawk's orange wings whirled as it circled the room. Morgan grabbed the keys with his left hand. He attempted to pull himself into a sitting position. As soon as he shuffled back, vertigo overwhelmed him.

He squeezed the keys in his fist, curled against his pillow and vomited. He gasped for air. The high wasp buzz vibrated past his ear, and he felt its prickling legs touch his closed fist. He shouted, jerked upright, and slammed his fist against the mattress. The tarantula hawk soared again.

Morgan forced himself to flip onto his knees. His fingers trembled as he attempted to get the key into the handcuffs. It wasn't working. Too big.

It's the wrong key! His own thoughts sounded as if they were drowning in mud. *There're two keys!*

The wasp landed on the handcuffs. Monstrous eyes glared. In Morgan's feverish vision, the creature's antennae seemed to curl into endless spirals. The hawk stabbed its abdomen down. Morgan stretched his wrist aside as the needle of its stinger extended.

He dropped the keys. The bronze wings thundered against the numb fingers of his right hand.

Morgan shouted and snatched the tarantula hawk by the head. He pinched. Crushed.

Between his fingers, the bug's head popped like a stale grape.

Bronze wings slackened. The headless wasp collapsed onto his pillow. Its abdomen continued to thrust. The stinger poked in and out, in and out, until at last, the metallic blue husk fell still.

Morgan shuddered and panted. He wiped insect goo onto his pillow. The bedroom had become a diseased carousel. He ignored the twisting vertigo and slid his fingers through the sheets. At last, he found the keys and determined that the smaller of the two fit the handcuffs.

"Well done, Morgan."

Pins and needles jabbed painfully through his right hand as the cuffs released. He rolled off the bed and crashed onto the hardwood floor. The ceiling above blurred winter white. "No!" He forced himself to his knees and crawled toward the dresser.

"You're a magnificent survivor," Chen said.

Morgan used every ounce of concentration to grab the edge of the dresser and pull himself up. He clutched the metal lockbox and pulled it down onto the floor next to him. The box flipped and rattled.

"Careful," Chen said. "The clock is ticking."

Morgan sucked in another breath. He found the larger key and fumbled until it fit into the padlock. The chrome lock snapped free, and he removed it.

His fingers trembled. *How the hell am I going to inject my heart like this,* he thought. He buried the thought. *You can do it. You can do this. Steady fingers . . .*

"Of course, nature is cruel," Chen said.

Morgan flipped the lid.

There was no syringe. No cure.

Instead, out poured three more tarantula hawks. Their rusty wings sliced the air. They drifted like small, dark angels.

Morgan howled with despair.

"Now you know how my daughter felt," came Chen's voice. "Such false hope."

Agony bloomed on Morgan's neck. His hand. His chest—*right* over his heart.

"Once you're gone, the remaining shareholders will restore my research, and something new—better—will be born of this horror."

Pain overpowered all other symptoms of Dr. Chen's poison.

"Of course, if there are more tarantulas prowling the top of your company," Dr. Chen said. "I know how to deal with them."

Morgan felt nothing but agony now. He screamed and screamed.

RADISH HUNTING
Melinda Brasher

S abine lifted the rifle, holding the pygmy deer steady in her sights. The animal raised its sleek head, black-edged ears twitching. Sabine's mouth watered. It wouldn't taste like beef—nothing here ever did—but at least it would be real meat. Her finger didn't hesitate on the trigger, but the rifle kicked back hard, and the creature leapt smoothly off into the woods.

"Should you really be out hunting?" Ryan asked when she dragged in later, empty-handed. "In your condition?"

Sabine sneered. That was his idea of being forceful. "I have four months to go." But it seemed like forever until she could get this nutrient-hogging baby out of her.

Children were expedient for the survival of the colony, and at thirty-four, Sabine still had a good ten or fifteen child-bearing years. Ryan understood that and had consented easily to the union. Especially after she wore a few form-fitting dresses and batted her eyes at him. Men—and boys—were so predictable. They'd married on his eighteenth birthday.

She would have preferred Edwin. Edwin could grow a beard without trying. But Ryan had a farm boy tan and farm boy muscles, and he would have been satisfactory even if he weren't the only available option.

She timed their efforts against her menstrual cycle. She took all the right vitamin supplements. Still it took eight months before she became pregnant. Her success pleased her at first. Now all she felt toward this bump on her belly was annoyance.

It had nauseated her for weeks. It interfered with work. Soon it would interfere with things like walking and sitting. Worst of all, it made her crave beef so badly she'd even cried once with the despair of it, ridiculous hormonal tears she felt helpless against. Because she'd never have real beef again. The two years she'd gone without were nothing compared to the eternity that stretched ahead.

She often dreamed about it. Steak, mostly. Slabs so thick the tines of her fork lost themselves in the red flesh. Back home her colleagues called her a fake vegetarian. "Pragmatic vegetarian," she used to correct. She wasn't afraid to eat a little turkey or chicken. She'd even had red meat a handful of times in the ten years since she turned vegetarian. It was about a balanced and healthy lifestyle, not ridiculous taboos.

"I made chicken," Ryan said hopefully, as if that would appease her. "With gravy and spiny greens." He was always falling over himself trying to get her anything she wanted. The fool probably still hoped she'd fall in love with him.

She raised an eyebrow. "You made *chicken*?"

None of the chickens they'd brought along on the ships had adapted to weightlessness. Some instinct kicked in and not one hen laid another egg. By the time they landed, only two scrawny hens remained, elderly and unable to adjust anew to the gravity of New Eden. So the colony made soup.

"Chicken?" she demanded.

"Well...drabchicken."

Chubby, flightless birds so ugly they made real chickens look like peacocks, with meat drabber than their feathers and chewy no matter how you cooked it, though Ryan kept trying in his clumsy way to dress it up like beef.

Sabine shrugged. "It's protein." But the gravy nauseated her and spiny greens always went slimy when cooked long enough to soften their spines. She pushed her plate away after a few bites.

Ryan sighed. "I'll go out to the bluffs tomorrow. Edwin said he saw a herd of unicorns there last week."

"*Gazella unicornis,*" she corrected. They were closer to gazelles than anything else. So what if they only had one horn? They certainly weren't pretty white fairytale horses. It drove her crazy to hear men like Edwin use the term. They'd already named the jabbers after a monster in a nonsense poem. As soon as they found a big lizard they'd probably start calling it a dragon. They were all crazy.

"You like their meat, don't you?" Ryan asked.

It was gamey and too lean, but better than most anything else they'd found. She shrugged.

He packed the next morning before sunup. "Off to get you some radishes," he said cheerfully.

"I don't want radishes. I want beef."

"Didn't your mother ever read you fairy tales?"

"What does that—"

"No, of course she didn't. Don't worry. I won't let the witch catch me." He filled his canteen and grabbed his pack.

"I'm going along."

"You've got to take care of yourself." But he reached a hand to her stomach and didn't look at the rest of her. Maybe he'd finally given up and turned all his attentions to his son.

Sabine shoveled provisions into a bag. "I'm going. Just try and stop me."

He gave in. He always did. They hardly talked during the bumpy journey. Normally that was preferable. The subtleties of farming never failed to bore her.

"Look," he whispered finally.

A whole herd of gazelles grazed off to the left. Their buff coats nearly hid them against the rocks, but their single black horns tore slashes in the landscape, and the white stripes on their faces glowed like eyes in the weak morning light as they stared placidly at her. She knew from previous expeditions that the creatures would bolt if startled, or if she and Ryan drew too close, but they hadn't yet learned an appropriate level of fear for this newest predator of theirs: man.

Ryan turned off the engine, put a finger to his lips, and slipped after them on foot. They weren't quite in range of the hunting rifles. The animals watched for a moment, then one by one went back to their meal. She and Ryan crept through the trees, edging closer to the meat-dotted meadow.

She stumbled. Their heads shot up, ears pricked. The closest one turned, its slender four-foot-long horn aimed so exactly at her that it seemed to disappear. She raised her gun.

"Not yet," Ryan whispered.

Its front hooves scratched the ground. Didn't the silly creature know it was more deer than bull? The crosshairs jerked around in front of her eyes. She steadied one arm against the trunk of a tree and pulled the trigger.

The shot echoed against the bluffs, but the herd didn't scatter. Twenty sets of eyes stared at her. Then one beast, bigger than the rest, moved his head slowly side to side, his gaze sweeping the rest of the herd. Several other creatures jerked their heads in rough half circles. The big gazelle turned back and dipped its nose slightly, its horn pointed right at her. Silence crowded the space between them. Then the beast pawed twice at the ground, lowered his body slightly, and charged. For a moment she simply watched the strength manifested in that run. Then the other creatures all bowed their heads and followed their leader into the stampede.

"Run!" Ryan yelled.

She didn't. She lifted her rifle and fired at the leader. The shot went wide. The animal zagged left, swung right, and kept coming. A third shot screamed past her, from Ryan's surer gun. Still the beast charged, its demon eyes trained on her. She scrambled backwards, tripped, and came down hard. The rifle skittered out of her hands. Ryan's went off again, four times in a row. One beast fell. Another. Sabine grabbed her rifle.

"Run!" Ryan screamed. He clamped down on her arm and tugged her backwards. They fled, stumbling over roots and crashing through bushes, away from the beasts but not quite in the direction of their vehicle.

"Where?" she gasped. They'd never be able to outrun the fleet-footed gazelles.

"There!" Ryan pointed. Half covered by the leaves of a spreading tree stood a wooden structure, a tiny platform on stilts, ten feet off the ground. "Up, up." He said, shoving her towards the ladder which was steep and rough to climb, and then turned to face their pursuers. Eight more shots shattered the air before she made it to the top.

Sabine fumbled with her gun. "I'll cover you," she yelled down at Ryan, punctuating her words with her own wayward bullet. Ryan pulled himself up just as the first beast reached the base of the ladder. She hooked her arm around one of the posts at the four corners, so if Ryan bumped her she wouldn't fall and impale herself on one of the gathering horns. She shot almost straight down, catching one in the forehead. It collapsed.

Another, smaller and darker, put its front hoofs up on the first rung.

"They can't climb, can they?"

Ryan stared, the tip of his rifle wobbling in distraction. "They never have before."

"Well, it's trying now." She aimed at its nose.

"Wait." Ryan pushed the barrel away. "What if…what if they're learning?"

"Then we'd better kill them quickly."

"What if they're intelligent?"

"A wolf's intelligent too." She knocked his hand away, aimed and fired. No more intelligent unicorn.

A noise rose from the others, ugly and guttural, like an old man clearing his throat. Then Ryan screamed. She whirled toward him as he swung the butt of his rifle down hard on the eight inches of glistening-sharp horn that stuck up through a gap in the boards below, right through his blood-spattered boot. She couldn't move. He screamed again when his gun made contact, but the horn withdrew and he stumbled backwards, nearly toppling off the platform. The bloody horn rammed through another gap between the boards, ten deadly inches this time. Another horn spiked up, so close it slid between her cuff and her ankle. She ripped herself away from it, found a solid-looking plank, grabbed a corner post, and leaned over the edge, cursing them in all the languages she knew, while she sighted one-handed and fired at the two below. They didn't even flinch but kept jabbing their horns up through the platform. Another joined in.

Ryan's weapon went off and the newcomer fell. There had to be a dozen left, most prowling the base of the ladder, and for a moment it seemed entirely possible they'd figure out how to use it. One saw her. Eyes glinting, it jumped up. She swung out of the way of its devil horn and aimed. It screamed as it fell. Or maybe that was Ryan.

She fired again and again. Everything disappeared around her but the dizzying flashes of animal flesh through the crosshairs. Her ears rang.

"Sabine, it's over," came a fuzzy voice. She swung her throbbing head side to side, scanning the ground below. Nothing moved. She turned to

139

Ryan, where he hunched over his gushing foot, cradling his left arm, where more blood dripped from a gash that ran nearly from his elbow to his wrist.

He reached out a hand to her. "Steady," he said. "Are you hurt?"

She shook her head. The fool was flooding the platform with scarlet, yet here he was asking about *her*.

She slammed down her rifle, splashing blood up her arm, then fumbled with the laces on his boot. He grunted when she yanked it off. "Hold it tight," she commanded. He obeyed, wrapping his strong hand around the fountain of blood.

She struggled out of her jacket, then tied it around the wound. Blood darkened the fabric almost immediately. She kept her hand pressed against it as she examined his arm. The cut ran long but not so deep.

"I'm going to get you out of here, to the biolab." She took one last look around. A couple of the creatures bleated feebly, not quite dead, but none would stop her now. And when she got Ryan to safety, she'd eat a steak made from every last one of the beasts.

He was breathing quickly now and sweating. Shock.

"Rest for a minute first." She eased him onto his back. There was nothing to prop his legs on, so she pulled them into her lap, while she kept her hand pressed hard against the wound.

A woman named Elizabeth was the head of their hospital, but she wasn't a real doctor. Her biolab was, at best, a poor shadow of an infirmary. If Ryan didn't bleed to death, would she even be able to fix his foot? The horn had stabbed right through the sole of his boot. It would have done far worse to fragile flesh. All this because she wanted beef.

"We got your radishes," Ryan said. His lips lacked color.

She glared down at his seeping foot. "Who built this? How did you know where to find it?"

"Dustin and the others made several of them last year."

"Well they didn't do a very good job. Not when it's beasts with four-foot horns and no fear that are hunting *you.*"

"I've never heard of them doing anything like this. I think they're smarter than we give them credit for."

"But look who survived," she said.

140

He frowned. "For now. There're pain pills in the med kit in the tractor cart. Maybe we should go." His breathing had evened out. He didn't seem disoriented.

"Fine." She pressed his rifle back into his hands. "Shoot anything that moves."

She made good time to the tractor cart, drove back to the blind, then climbed up to where Ryan lay with his arms wrapped around the gun, semi-conscious. She slapped his face just hard enough to rouse him, then maneuvered his clumsy body down the ladder and through the lumps of dead gazelle which circled the platform.

It wasn't really a road—just a path, a fading scar across the plain, rutted and crowded in with brush. Safer to keep both hands on the wheel. Ryan squirmed in the hard seat next to her, moaning against the pain. What he needed were stronger drugs and a good doctor. What he had was her. She slipped one hand off the wheel, over to his. It would do absolutely no good. Still, she squeezed softly and his head twisted over to her. She gripped the wheel harder with her one hand and stared straight ahead.

Sabine hauled in more meat than they could process before it began to rot. The whole colony reeked of it for days.

Ryan wouldn't eat it, even when he woke up ravenous after the surgery. Neither would most of the others, once they heard the story. Elizabeth blathered on about wanting to study the beasts, to determine how intelligent they really were, to try communicating with them, making peace. Sabine didn't even point out their sentimental folly. Instead, she spent her energy trying to take care of Ryan's fields while he recovered.

Each evening, after a long day of sun and dirt and crops, she found a rock or a fallen log, away from the eyes of the colony, and rested her feet, swollen from the work or the pregnancy. Each evening, she lit a fire and pulled out the now blackened grill. And each evening, she wondered what her colleagues back on Earth would think of her, sitting alone under a darkening sky, devouring pounds of barbecued unicorn steak.

CROCOPORK
Liam Hogan

From the rooftop I squint along the sights, lining up a sow sunning herself in the thin sunlight. I can almost taste her buttery flesh, flash fried in a pan...

I don't squeeze the trigger. There's no point. It's too warm and I don't have the ammo to waste.

I hardly have any ammo at all.

The fat sow is not alone. Far from it. There are a hundred of the monsters gathered round the research centre, maybe more. Not doing much, not yet. A few are wallowing in mud hollows with contented little grunts and squeals, but most of them are still asleep, waiting for the last of the morning mist to burn off. By noon it'll be a riot of boisterous behaviour. By then I'll be back in the bowels of the research centre, trying my best to block out the god-awful noise.

Something draws them here like flies and I have the sneaking impression that the 'something' is me.

We had one once. A crocopig that is, I'm not talking about Crocopork. Everybody had Crocopork! No, we had a crocopiglet called Winston as the unofficial company mascot. I got him on the black market so we had to keep him out of sight of the CO. That was in the early days of course.

Winston wasn't pretty—pretty evil looking, actually—but he was well behaved and as smart as a whip. I grew up on a farm, in deepest darkest Somerset, so I was used to all sorts of animals, all kinds of pets. Winston was faster to housetrain than any dog I ever owned, which was a good thing when we were trying to keep a beast his size hidden.

It was on a trip back to the family farm, on my first furlough after Basic, that I acquired the little blighter. I wouldn't have been able to afford him if the Department of Agriculture hadn't bought Da's farm and

142

if he hadn't been feeling unusually generous with the proceeds, courtesy of the almost full bottle of aged single malt whisky I'd smuggled out of the officer's mess. Or maybe the old skinflint would have given me the money anyway, seeing as to how it was kind of my inheritance.

I guess my Da got out of poultry at just the right time. Who knew that you'd never want to eat chicken again?

Defra didn't say what they were planning to do with Dad's land and he didn't ask, as they were paying well over the odds. They even bought all his livestock, which was strange, but Da wasn't complaining. Thing is, I don't think he'd have sold at all if I'd agreed to follow in his size eleven footsteps and hadn't run off to join the Army instead.

Even in the three days I was home, the amount of steel and concrete and barbed wire they shipped past Da's now-farmless-farmhouse told me something was up. But all I got from an idle query to a girl in Council Planning I'd once dated was that they were building a 'Secure Research Centre for New Breeds'.

'Species' would have been more accurate.

'Nemesis' even more so.

When I was offered a mewling Winston by a dodgy-looking character in the Bull and Finch, it was the first time I'd seen one, but by then I'd heard the rumours. What started out as whispers—that it ate anything, even garbage, that it put on weight three times faster than a pig and bred like rabbits—turned into beer-fuelled debate on how much of it was hot air and what it would mean for the traditional farmers if any of it was true.

"Ah," thundered Old Man McClintock, his pint of mild slopping over the peeling varnish of the faded wooden bar. "But what does it *taste* like?"

A small voice at my shoulder murmured: "Tastes bloody fantastic. Want to see one?"

It was the aforementioned dodgy-looking character.

I guess he worked at the Centre. I don't see how else he could have got his hands on Winston. I don't know if he knew who I was, if he knew that the Centre was being built on my Dad's land, or if he just thought I was one of the younger, and therefore more gullible, farmers. I certainly wasn't the only one in the pub wearing camo trousers. He must have thought the chance to own one was irresistible; the amount he tried to extort from me. You could have bought a half decent motorbike for what he was asking.

Once we'd settled on a more realistic price, which was still a fair chunk of an arm and leg and pretty much wiped out what my Da had given me, I asked him what to feed the ugly little beast.

He scratched his head. "Milk, I guess. Though in about a week, he'll eat anything. They seem quite partial to chicken."

"Chicken?" I asked, suddenly wondering if that was what had happened to Dad's livestock.

He nodded, amused. "Right down to the beak: bones, feathers, guts, and all. No waste. Cleanest eaters I've ever seen."

I looked down at the little snout and its array of just-emerging razor-sharp teeth and asked a question you might not have expected from a fifteen-stone buzz cut squaddie.

"Is it safe?" I asked.

"Safe?" he laughed, "'Course it's safe. He wouldn't hurt a fly."

When I showed Winston to my Da he was less than impressed. "If I'd've known you were gonna throw my money away..." he shook his head. "What the hell use is *that*?"

Truth was I hadn't thought that far ahead. I usually didn't, much to Sarge's ire. "*Think*, McKye!" he would fume. "Think things through, for Chrissakes!"

I shrugged. "I thought you might need a pet, now that you're a man of leisure."

"Ha bloody ha. If it's all right with you son, you can bloody well keep him. Ugly bloody thing."

Which was how Winston came to be our company mascot.

We'd had him for about four months when Defra finally got around to announcing the worst kept secret in agricultural history. They did it in grand style though. They booked a top London hotel and invited celebrity chefs and food critics, all of whom agreed that Crocopork was, as the accursed jingle in my head repeats ad nauseam: 'the best meat, you'll ever eat'.

We watched it on the big screen in the mess tent, cheering every time a crocopig appeared on the screen, everyone raising their pints and toasting 'Winston!' much to Sarge's bemusement.

144

They paraded a gaggle of eco-scientists claiming that, because Crocopork farming had a lower carbon footprint than other meat production (even poultry), it would help save the planet. And they had Dr Walter 'Frankenstein' Sneed, the crocopig inventor, being interviewed live.

He'd just been asked the obvious question: how do you make a crocopig? Which seemed pointless, because everyone *knew* it was a hybrid of a crocodile and a pig. But Dr Sneed waved his champagne glass around and said that it wasn't that simple, that things can't be grafted together without an intermediary, some common stock, an extra ingredient. It was while he was being asked what *else* was in a crocopig that the man from the Ministry hastily intervened.

"I'm sorry to interrupt, Dr Sneed," he said, as he elbowed the doc aside and waved a sheet of paper at the camera, "But we've been getting reports that there are members of the public who seem to have acquired crocopigs as, well, remarkably, as pets."

That got another resounding "Winston!" cheer and I began to worry Sarge would twig.

The Ministry man continued: "I'm not sure where they got them from but it's as good a time as any to announce that the Department for Environment, Food and Rural Affairs has ruled that as a GM foodstuff, all crocopig farms are licensed by Defra and have to meet strict regulations to prevent any crocopigs being released into the open.

"In addition, under the Dangerous Animals Act, anyone who does have one as a pet will be forced to surrender it to Defra immediately or face a five-year prison sentence."

There was a chorus of *ooh*s and a couple of sharp digs to my ribs, which I did my best to ignore.

"And... *are* they dangerous?" the reporter nervously asked.

"Not at all," the man from the Ministry beamed. "They're more docile than sheep. However history is littered with supposedly benign species being let loose in the wild and the havoc they have accidentally caused, such as rats on the Galapagos Islands and rabbits in Australia. We are merely taking sensible precautions."

I was sad to say goodbye to Winston, even if he wasn't quite the little bundle of scales and claws he'd once been. By then he must have weighed close to six hundred pounds and he'd rapidly grown beyond what the scraps of even a whole company could sustain. Especially as after a hard day's exercises you tended to lick your plate clean, regardless of whatever slop you found yourself eating.

The mess hall cooks were even sadder. Winston had lived for the last month in one of the disused storerooms to the side of the kitchens, having outgrown the other hiding places we'd had for him.

"He loved my spag bol," one cook blubbed, giving him a hug, Winston's rasping tongue lapping at the sauce stains on his apron. "Never no complaints from my little Winston."

We managed to smuggle him off-base in the back of an army land rover. A couple of miles down the road I changed into civvies and transferred Winston to a waiting hire van, leaving Jack faking engine problems to await my return.

Dropping him off I stifled a tear as Winston scuttled happily towards the other animals in the hastily erected holding pens.

I didn't think the amnesty would work. Word from my Da was there were farmers making a lot of money breeding crocopigs and selling them on. But the pens were full when I dropped Winston off.

I spoke to a couple of the owners, who told strange tales of missing cats and even dogs. A few of the illegal breeders—busy releasing whole trailers full of crocosows and piglets—said they were scared of having their hands bitten off when they put out the feeding bowls.

That didn't mesh with my experience of Winston at all. Oh, he was scary *looking*, a fact we'd used to great effect on any new recruits that came our way, locking them in his crate overnight. But Winston was such a big, affectionate softy that I kind of ignored those warnings, stupid though that seems now.

Because those breeders had discovered what Defra and the first of the licensed crocopig farmers were only just waking up to. That while it was true that a single crocopig wouldn't say boo to a goose, once you got a few together they got bolder and more aggressive. The bigger the pack the bolder they got, until that goose was well and truly cooked.

The first human victim of the crocopigs was a Defra approved farmer called Alex Fettings, who was a bit late with the morning feed, about two months after we'd said goodbye to Winston. All they found of *him* was his horn-rimmed glasses. Caused a bit of an uproar, that did, but by then Crocopork was in every restaurant, supermarket and fridge in the country. Not to mention every mess hall and ration pack, so it was here to stay. Imports of Danish bacon and New Zealand lamb had dropped to record lows just as Crocopork exports were booming, providing a welcome fillip to the struggling post-Brexit economy.

No, the main concern of the Ministry at the time was meeting demand for the new wondermeat. That and investigating reports of crocopigs being smuggled abroad, to start up illicit farms in mainland Europe, the US, and even further afield.

The man from the Ministry said that Fetting's unfortunate demise was a freak accident, that perhaps he'd had a heart attack and fallen into the feeding trough. But Defra decided to close all the smaller-scale licensed crocopig farms anyway. In their place they opened huge government-run reservations with electric fences and automated abattoirs.

Which of course just brought more of the crocopigs together. Nobody realised quite how many there were in those facilities.

Not until they escaped, anyway.

The call came one bright autumn morning. The sort of crisp English day nothing bad could possibly happen. Ho hum.

"Got a job for you boys," the Captain said at the briefing. "Defra--"

"Ah crap," murmured Jack in my ear. "Another bloody Foot an' Mouth cleanup."

Jack had been in the TA back in 2001, when the outbreak had been at its peak, bulldozers shovelling culled animals into pyres in the middle of the field, smoke-blackened air thick with the stench of burning livestock drifting across the paralysed landscape.

I missed whatever the Captain had been saying next, but the slide that flickered onto the screen was clear enough. A full grown crocoboar, about the size Winston was when we shipped him out under a tarpaulin cover. Heck, it might even have been Winston, for all we knew.

"Crocopigs, Captain?" I asked, loudly, drowning out the stifled echo of his name.

The captain shot me a resigned look. "Yes, McKye. Crocopigs, as I've been saying. There's been a breakout and as they're registered as dangerous animals the Army has been asked to help."

"To do what, sir?" piped up another voice.

The captain gave a wry grin. "Why, to do what you bunch of lovely killers do best. To kill them."

The tent bubbled with excitement and the captain rode it for a moment before delivering the punch line. "The civilians have been cleared out of the area. We have full operational authority and we're going to run this as a live ammo training exercise."

"We're going to shoot them, sir?"

"Yes, Coogan. Shoot, stab, mortar, blow up. Whatever we see fit. But *mainly* shoot. Our mission is to contain and destroy every crocopig escapee. We have been asked in particular to prevent any crocopigs from reaching Yeovil, as we don't want to evacuate the whole bloody town."

Sam Coogan started grumbling. "Hardly a fair fight, Captain. Not unless we arm the critters first."

There was laughter at that until Sarge raised his arm. "Right, you lot, those animals are not going to catch themselves and the longer you take, the further they'll spread. Collect your weapons and ammunition from the Quartermaster. Vehicles leave in fifteen."

There was a hint of morning mist in the air as a fireteam of me, Coogan, Jack Whitey, and Baxter took a jeep down hedge-rowed lanes thick with blackberries, the rest of the company converging on the reservation from other points of the compass.

We were still a couple of miles from our destination when Whitey slapped me on the shoulder, pointed through a break in the hedge and yelled something over the rumble of the engine. Baxter, driving, must have heard or seen, because the jeep slew to a halt and I stood up in my seat to see what had caught their attention.

Across the field a cluster of black and white cows lay in the shade of a tree and I wondered if Baxter was going to make some fatuous remark about it being about the rain. A young calf ran past, full of energy, playing tag with a number of oddly squat, mottled brown heifers.

And then, as the calf made a squeal of terror, the picture rearranged itself in my head. The calf wasn't playing tag. It was being herded, the ring of heifers slowly tightening like a noose. The black and white cows under the tree were far too still and were lying at awkward, unnatural angles. And those heifers...

They weren't squatting, they were short legged. Way too short legged to be cows. With heads long and sharp, a long row of jagged teeth glittering in the sunshine.

Crocopigs.

Their savage game came to a rapid end. The circle of crocopigs closed and left the calf nowhere to run. As the pack surged forward the last pitiful scream snapped us out of our stupor.

"HQ, this is Charlie-7. Crocopigs sighted, over."

"Charlie-7, report your position."

Baxter read out the GPS coordinates and there was a pause before the radio operator stated the bleeding obvious. "Must be an outlying group."

"HQ, what are our instructions, over?"

The Captain's clipped voice rang out. "Congratulations, lads. You're going to be first to engage. Confirmed no other units in your vicinity. Let's see how sharp your shooting is—precision fire: try to be efficient. Report back number of kills for the cleanup squad."

"I hope the cleanup squad do a mean BBQ," joked Coogan, off radio, as we took up position. Baxter and Whitey headed along the hedge towards the other gate so that we had a wider angle of fire and could minimise the risk of a stampede.

I peered through the scope of the SA80 wondering if, when push came to shove, I'd be able to pull the trigger. After Winston it'd be like shooting a pet dog.

Even if those crocopigs were busy snorting and crunching on the corpses of cows.

It wasn't a pretty sight. They were great lumbering beasts, low to the ground, a body longer and narrower than a pig's, a head blunter than a crocodile's. The noises were none too pleasant either.

I guessed they'd been feasting for a while. Which was good news for us as it put them all within a smaller area of the field. Their position by the tree stood in a bit of a dip, so I motioned Coogan forward and up the rise, that way we'd have a better view. I heard Coogan utter "Eww!" as his crouched approach was halted by a cow pat, and I grinned.

It was the last grin I can remember making. When things went tits up, they went tits up fast.

149

We were waiting for Baxter and Whitey to get into position before starting the cull. My guess is, they never made it. A sudden burst of gun fire had us swinging our rifles into action.

"Goddamn glory boys," Coogan growled, drawing a line on the nearest crocopig, "they were supposed to wait."

But the crocopigs weren't falling dead or squealing in wounded anguish. Instead they were looking up inquisitively from their meal of raw cow.

"McKye! Coogan!" the radio squawked. "Crocopigs to North and... GODDAMN!"

There was a blast of crackly gunfire, echoed moments later as the sharp sound drifted over the field.

I looked at Coogan and Coogan looked at me, and then he stood up. I guess he did it to see what was happening on the other side of the hedge, but he was looking the other way when the crocopigs' attention shifted in our direction.

"Um, Coogan?" I shook his arm. "Back to the jeep, yeah?"

He nodded grimly and we backed away as a line of crocopigs formed and steadily advanced. The gunfire from the other side of the hedge became erratic and abruptly stopped.

"You drive," Coogan said, jumping into the back of the jeep as I dropped my rifle onto the front passenger seat.

We sped down the lane, Coogan training his rifle on the hole in the hedge we'd come through. As we pulled away he switched his aim to the front, leaning over the side of the jeep, though the curve of the road and the height of the hedges meant we couldn't see very far.

I resisted the temptation to slow down. After all, we were the ones with the guns.

We half expected to come across Baxter and Whitey sitting on top of a mound of carcasses, smiling triumphantly. The mound was there alright, but it was a living, moving thing, piglets squealing at the fringes with no sign of our two comrades.

Not unless you counted the ugly red smears on the crocopig snouts.

Coogan raised his rifle and began firing. Double taps—bang, bang, re-aim, then bang-bang again, making certain of each one. I reached for my rifle but he shook his head. "Back up," he hissed, "slow and steady."

The crocopig pack advanced down the lane, leaving behind a tattered mess in which two gore-slicked rifles were the only recognisable features. They came in a snarling wave, splitting and drifting, crossing and changing speed. While any single crocopig's movements seemed utterly random, the body of them somehow moved forward in a solid line, even as Coogan dropped them one by one.

I heard his rifle click empty and sped up a little as he stretched over the seat to pick up mine.

And that was when we passed the hole in hedge we'd been through earlier.

I'd never seen a crocopig move so fast: I didn't know they *could*. I heard the thunder of cloven hooves and then a tan shape leapt through the air, clattered as it clipped the side of the jeep but continued on, a meaty sledgehammer that folded Coogan in two and bowled him out of the jeep. I stepped on the accelerator as another came leaping towards me. The change of speed meant it caught and wiped out the windshield instead, crocopig and twisted metal and glass sliding cleanly off the bonnet as the lane filled with a tide of hungry beasts and the two groups of crocopigs merged and swelled, with already no trace of where Coogan had fallen.

"Shit, shit, shit!" I cursed. The flying boar had taken out the wing mirror as well. I was driving blind and in reverse. I needed to stop and turn round, stop and radio for help. Stop and bloody well throw up.

The country lane cut onto a proper road and I nearly took out a post van as I swung sharply round to follow it. The postie's horn honked as he swerved and I looked after his two-fingered salute in shock. So much for the area being clear.

I grabbed for the radio but when I clicked it on to make my report the airwaves were already full of shouting and firing and screaming, desperate orders to "fall back" and "maintain perimeters".

All hopeless, of course. There were estimates the crocopigs outnumbered the Army a thousand to one and most of our troops had never fired a rifle in anger in their short, sorry lives. A thousand to one! Do you know how much ammo the average soldier carries? Not enough, not *nearly* enough.

And dead soldier or dead crocopig, it didn't really matter to the millions of hungry crocopig survivors. Hungry survivors that grew fat and strong on the battlefield dead. Grew fat and strong and gave birth to dozens more ravenous little Winstons.

I didn't bother reporting my position, or calling for help. What was one lone voice, one lone soldier in the midst of that day's chaos? I switched the radio to the civilian channels and listened as the news reports gave the bigger picture, driving at random down country lanes in crisp bright sunshine as our world came to an end.

After picking the battlefield clean, the crocopigs moved onto the living. Early reports said they stripped Yeovil in less than four hours before moving on to the next town. And then the next, and the next, only slowing their advance to break through the fences of each crocopig reservation they came across, their numbers growing with every mile. Local radio swiftly fell silent. National radio began playing automated emergency broadcasts that warned everyone to take shelter, not to leave their homes. As if that would help.

The jeep coughed to an exhausted halt, fuel tank empty. I looked around in surprise. I don't know if it was by chance or by some instinct, but I'd pulled up in a pub car park. A pub I knew: The Bull and Finch.

For a moment, all was calm and I had a sense of safety, of being home.

I wondered if it was opening time yet.

The blast of a shotgun shattered my illusion and someone came through the frosted glass windows backwards. Old Man McClintock, wrestling the barrel of his gun from the toothy snout of an enraged crocopig.

By the time I reached for the rifle, the snout was wrapped around the old man's head and besides, it was empty. Coogan had taken my loaded rifle over the side of the jeep.

When I looked up from reloading, the crocopig had dragged its meal back into the dark of the pub lounge. I shuddered at the horrific noises emerging from the hole in the window, grabbed my pack and started running up the lane towards my Da's farmhouse.

I saw the hoof prints even before the flattened gate, before the trampled vegetable garden that was a new addition since my last visit, clocked the front door hanging by one hinge. Maybe if I'd still been in the jeep and still thought I could outpace a charging crocopig...

Maybe then I'd have stopped.

But I wasn't and so I didn't. I kept on running, towards the Research Centre built on Da's top field. You see, I knew—my Da being their neighbour—that the complex had been mothballed when the crocopigs were moved to the reservations. And I figured if there was one place that would keep a crocopig out, it was somewhere that had been built to keep a crocopig *in*.

Pretty smart, huh? How's *that* for thinking things through?

Sarge would be proud of me. "Lucky bastard, McKye", he would say, a wry grin on his weathered face, "You lucky son of a bitch."

I didn't expect to still be here, half a year later, lining up targets I can't afford to shoot. The cavalry never arrived. It's a good thing Defra left behind a lot of food.

It's mostly tinned Crocopork products, which is kind of funny, kinda ironic. Sometimes you just have to look at things with a positive spin.

So yes, maybe I am surrounded by four massive concrete and steel walls, topped by razor-sharp barbed wire. But it's not *me* in the cage, it's everything outside of these walls.

That's what I say to myself.

I keep myself busy. Improvise, adapt, and overcome, right? Or survive, at least. I've rigged up water collectors from the gutters and I'm trying to grow a few crops to supplement my dwindling supply of canned fruit and veg. If—*when*—that runs out, I guess I'll have to venture beyond these twelve foot barricades.

I'll take my rifle and I'll pick a cold winter's day. Crocopigs are sluggish then; it must be the reptile in them. But I haven't dared to do so yet.

I have this reoccurring dream. Or rather, nightmare. I'm back in my Da's farmhouse looking through the empty cupboards for something to eat, when I hear a noise and I go into the living room thinking it might be Da. There, curled up in front of the TV with the remote in its claw, is a huge crocoboar I just *know* is a fully grown Winston.

He rears up, the armoured scales on his belly rippling as the solid muscular bulk moves, his claws skitter against the lampshade and, as I stare into an ever-widening maw and dark shadows tilt crazily from side to side...

It's about then that I wake up drenched in sweat and gasping for breath.

So no, I haven't been out yet.

There's a panoramic viewing window in one of the high walls. I guess it was built to let the scientists see in, but now it lets me look out. I sat there for hours in the early days, waiting for a rescue that never came.

I don't bother much anymore. The skies have gone clear of contrails and you can see the stars. So many stars! Which tells me more than I want to know about the fate of mankind, and what happened to all those smuggled out crocopigs across Europe and the rest of the world.

Occasionally a satellite will pass overhead and I'll wonder if it still talks to anyone down here. Or I'll spot the International Space Station, its solar wings catching the evening sun. Are there still astronauts up there, waiting for a ride home that will never come?

I haven't seen another human being for... seven months now, not since Old Man McClintock. But every so often I'll get the feeling that I'm being watched and I'll look up to see a family of crocopigs on the other side of the viewing window.

I thought at first that they were trying to get in, that they were hungry, that they'd eaten everything and everyone beyond the walls and had finally come for me. But they never do anything except watch.

Oh, the kids might run around a bit, the mother trying her best to control them. Perhaps one of the little ones will hold a thigh bone with those amazingly dextrous claws and suck on it like it was an ice-cream. Maybe the father will stand upright to get a better view, or sharply tap on the glass if I'm asleep or too static.

If I had Dr. Sneed here, the 'Father of the Crocopig', I'd ask him—just before I threw him to his waiting, ravenous, bastard offspring—just *what* extra genetic component he'd used to splice a crocodile and a pig together. What extra element makes the crocopig so damned smart, so quick to adapt and so very, very dangerous.

But he's not here. It's just me and those ever-watching crocopigs.

So I guess I'll never know.

Thank you for reading! If you like the book, please leave a review on Amazon and Goodreads. Even if you don't like it, please still leave a review.

To keep up with more Nightmare Press news, join the Anubis Press Dynasty on Facebook.

Now that the anthology is over and you have somehow survived the uprising, do you feel like there is something missing? Does it seem like something important was forgotten? Have you asked yourself that all-important question yet?

Which question?

You know which question.

Where are the cats?

Well, we did have a lion.

But that doesn't count, you say? Where are the little domesticated monsters that are loveable but moody?

Why, you can't have an animal horror collection without the ever-dangerous feline.

Yes – they seem to be missing. But, don't worry – they are coming.

Oh yes, they are coming.

Get ready.

Prepare yourself to soon be

SCRATCHED...

ABOUT THE AUTHORS

MICHELLE MELLON

Michelle Mellon has been published in nearly a dozen horror and science fiction anthologies. In August 2015, she and her husband relocated from San Francisco to Germany, where Ms. Mellon was a stay-at-home mom to their cat while working on her recently released horror story collection. She currently works for a software startup and is nearing completion of her second story collection.

Learn more about her work at mpmellon.com

DAVID TURTON

David Turton is an author of dark fiction and horror. He has penned several short stories which have been published in magazines and anthologies.

David was born in Yorkshire and graduated with a degree in Journalism. He now lives by the sea in the North East of England.

Learn more about his work at davidturtonauthor.wordpress.com

PATRICK WINTERS

Patrick Winters is a graduate of Illinois College in Jacksonville, IL, where he earned a degree in English Literature and Creative Writing. He has been published in the likes of *Sanitarium Magazine*, *Deadman's Tome*, *Trysts of Fate*, and other such titles.

A full list of his previous publications may be found at his author's site, if you are so inclined to know:

http://wintersauthor.azurewebsites.net/Publications/List

M.R. DELUCA

M.R. Deluca has short stories published in *Shadows in Salem*, *After the Happily Ever After*, *O Horrid Night*, and *Strangely Funny V*. In addition to the beauty of words, M.R. enjoys numbers, speleothems, and homemade whoopie pies.

STANLEY B. WEBB

Stanley is a resident of New York State. He and his family live in an antique farm house near Lake Ontario. Stanley wasted much of his youth watching monster movies, reading science fiction, drawing pictures and writing stories. Many of his tales have appeared in magazines and anthologies, including Gypsum Sound Tales' "COLP: A Little Bit of Nonsense", "Haunted life" from Alban Lake Publishing, and "Starship Logs" from Tell-Tale Press. His bibliography may be viewed on his website at stanleybwebbauthor.wordpress.com, or his Author Central page at amazon.com/author/stanleywebb.

Stanley thanks everyone who has ever read his work.

REBECCA GRANSDEN

Rebecca Gransden is a writer from an island in the United Kingdom. Her work is published or forthcoming at X-R-A-Y, Burning House Press, Anti-Heroin Chic, Five:2:One, and Planet Scumm, among others. The novel Anemogram and short story collection Rusticles are available everywhere.

Find her online at rebeccagransden.wordpress.com

JACOB FLOYD

Jacob Floyd is one half of the Frightening Floyds, with his wife Jenny. Together they write paranormal nonfiction and have two ghost walks in Kentucky (*Shepherdsville History and Haunts Tour* and *NuLu History and Haunts Tour*). You can find them on Facebook under The Frightening Floyds, and you can follow their tours at their respective pages. They also own and operate Anubis Press, Nightmare Press, and Wild West Press.

Jacob is also a horror author who wrote *Night of the Possums*. He is also a big fan of Alfred Hitchcock. You can follow him on Facebook, Twitter, Instagram, Tumblr, and at his blog, *Jacob Floyd's Ghosts and Monsters*.

JUDITH BARON

Judith Baron's short stories have been published in Future Visions Anthologies: Volume 2, Horror Bites Magazine Issue #8, The Poet's Haven Digest: It Was a Dark & Stormy Night, Trembling With Fear and Spadina Literary Review, and will appear in Colors In Darkness: Deadly Bargain and Canadian Dreadful Anthology in 2019.

You can find her at judithbaron.wixsite.com.

KENNETH BYKERK

Kenneth Bykerk lives in the ghost town of Howells, Arizona, the suburb of the ghost town of Walker, AZ on the creek where the gold was found that brought recognition of Territorial status to the land. His days spent free from the real world often find him hiking through the ruins and forgotten graveyards that surround his mountain home. Experiencing the first of hopefully many 2nd childhoods, he has taken to writing down the musings inspired by his hikes to lost mines or his midnight strolls through the remains of Howells. "Child of the Earth" is one of 33 stories he has produced these last four years. These 33 stories are collectively known as *The Tales of the Bajazid.*

Other than "Child of the Earth", four others have been sold with one, "Kachina", appearing in the February 2018 issue of *WeirdBook* #38 and, "Mercy Holds No Measure" in the upcoming *WeirdBook 2018* annual. "Where Lies Hope" appears in the November 2018 issue of *WeirdMask* and "The Woman in the Tree" in Tell-Tale Press 2018 Winter Holidays edition, *The Blood Tomes.*

The Tales of the Bajazid chronicles the history of one of the many ghost towns in the mountains of central Arizona. One day while showing a friend the ruins of the smelter walking distance down the creek, he was asked why so much concrete was used to seal the entrance. The ruins he had played upon as a child, that his grandmother had played upon as a child, transformed before his eyes as each collapsed and hidden adit or old shaft hopefully filled began telling stories only he could hear. Following the advice of write what you know, with his changed perspective, those places he played as a child still serve to inspire hours of time lost to forest trails but now in ways that child of yore would probably be disturbed by. That kid was a scaredy-cat.

J.T. HAVEN

Walking the fine line between humor/offense, speculation/reality, and love/fear, author and poet J.T. Haven's "why" for writing—and living—is connection. This quirky writer's *Splintered Musings* writing prompt book series fosters connections between herself/readers, fellow writers/their muses, and the world/our universal imagination. Haven's work—whether poetry, prose, or splintered musing—is always penned from a place of authenticity and exploration. As a writer in the Bountiful Balcony Books family, you can find out more about J.T. Haven and her work at www.bountifulbalconybooks.com/jthaven or on social media as @jthavenwriter.

HANNAH SHANNON

Hannah Shannon is an author and illustrator. Some of her other work includes *Succ You (Murderotica)*, *Inspiration: Inspiring Coloring Pages for Adults*, *Prelude to Weird: PG Coloring Pages for the Wild at Heart,* as well as *Breaking the Boy* and *Savage Fascination* with Janine Wilde. You can check out her work at Amazon, as well as on Facebook at Hannahshannonillustrator.

KEVIN FOLLIARD

Kevin M. Folliard is a Chicagoland writer whose published fiction includes scary stories collections *Christmas Terror Tales* and *Valentine Terror Tales*, and adventure novels such as *Matt Palmer and the Komodo Uprising*. His work has also been collected by The Horror Tree, Flame Tree Publishing, Hinnom Magazine, and more.

You can keep up with Kevin at kevinfolliard.com

MELINDA BRASHER

Melinda Brasher spends her time writing fiction, traveling, and teaching English as a second language in places like Poland, Mexico, the Czech Republic, and Arizona. Her talents include navigating by old-fashioned map, combining up to three languages in a single incomprehensible sentence, and dealing cards really, really fast. Her short fiction and travel writing appear in *Pseudopod*, *Intergalactic Medicine Show*, *Nous*, and others.

Visit her online at www.melindabrasher.com or @MelindaJBrasher

LIAM HOGAN

Liam Hogan is a London based, award winning short story writer (Quantum Shorts 2015 & Roswell Award 2016). With short stories in around 40 anthologies, his twisted fantasy collection *Happy Ending NOT Guaranteed* is out now!

The night of the possums began on a chilly autumn morning around 2am in late October.

On a dark country road, a young man is torn to shreds by wild animals. The news of his grisly death rocks the town. When a similar death occurs later that day, the town is in the grips of fear.

In rural Bardstown, Kentucky, opossums have risen up against the populace. People are being maimed and devoured throughout the city. These are not your ordinary opossums, either: they are smarter, stronger, faster, and far more vicious—some larger than any opossum anyone has ever seen, growing as long as four feet and as heavy as fifty pounds, with teeth capable of cleaving bone.

As the flesh-eating scourge quickly spreads from one end of Bardstown to the other, a few of those who survived the attacks band together in an attempt to eradicate the maniac marsupials. But, the number of the beasts grows by the hour and the force becomes too insurmountable and the survivors soon realize escape is their only option.

But, beyond the berserk behavior of the carnivorous creatures is a darker secret—something ancient and unnatural that threatens all those who are bitten. Before anyone can find out what is driving these opossums to kill, the survivors must battle their way through the merciless onslaught of claws and teeth and leave the threat of Bardstown behind them.

Explore the dark side of Tinseltown in this collection of paranormal stories, conspiracy theories, curses, and legends about some of Hollywood's most iconic names: Marilyn Monroe, Rudolph Valentino, Charlie Chaplin, James Dean, Jean Harlow, Clark and Carole, Lucille Ball, Michael Jackson, Bela Lugosi, Lon Cheney, John Belushi, and the King himself—Elvis Presley—and many more. Join the Frightening Floyds as they take you on a terrifying journey through the city of glamour and glitz!

Available on Amazon in paperback and Kindle!

Thank you for reading! If you like the book, please leave a review on Amazon and Goodreads. Even if you don't like it, please still leave a review.

To keep up with more Nightmare Press news, join the Anubis Press Dynasty on Facebook.